A Boy for
a Man's Job

A Boy for a Man's Job

The Story of the Founding of St. Louis

By N I N A   B R O W N   B A K E R

Illustrated by Edward F. Cortese

WINSTON
ADVENTURE
BOOKS

Cecile Matschat, Editor
Carl Carmer, Consulting Editor

THE JOHN C. WINSTON COMPANY

Philadelphia · Toronto

Made in the United States of America
L. C. Card #52-5892

The Birth of a City

On the west bank of the Mississippi River stands St. Louis, Missouri—one of the largest cities of the United States, the biggest between Chicago and the Pacific Coast. Looking at present-day St. Louis—with its beautiful parks, miles of streets, thousands of homes, and almost a million inhabitants—who would think that less than two hundred years ago St. Louis did not exist, was only a grove of walnut trees on a high bluff overlooking a lonely river.

Yet it was there, in 1764, that a fourteen-year-old boy, Auguste Chouteau, and his faithful "thirty" laid the foundation for this great American city. How he did it and why is the basis for this true but little-known story.

Auguste's stepfather, Pierre Laclede Liguest, for reasons apparently unknown, upon reaching Louisiana some years previous, had discarded his surname and called himself merely Pierre Laclede. Unable to make a satisfactory living in New Orleans for the family he had acquired in the New World, Pierre decided to build a fur-trading post far up the Mississippi. This not only would be a profitable venture for Maxent and Company, but it would mean a junior partnership for Pierre. Further, he would be able to live the wild, free life he preferred.

The site Pierre selected was one previously occupied by a Jesuit mission, abandoned early in the century. This was probably the first settlement in what is now Missouri. But the first permanent settlement was that established by Auguste, and named for the sainted Louis IX of France.

From the beginning the project was successful. In a few years, Maxent, Laclede and Company had monopolies on the fur trade of more than two dozen Indian nations. The Post soon became the chief outfitting point for expeditions to the north and west. Colonists came in ever-increasing numbers, preferring the feeble rule of Spain to that of Britain.

From that time to the present, the expansion of St. Louis has been rapid, until now it is one of America's great cities—a city built by a dream, a boy, and the faithful "thirty."

CECILE MATSCHAT, *Editor*
CARL CARMER, *Consulting Editor*

CONTENTS

CHAPTER   PAGE

The Birth of a City v

1. "A Boy Should Be Beaten!" . . . 1

2. "You Are Not to Go" 16

3. Alone on the River 33

4. The Boys Find Their Job 48

5. At Ste. Geneviève 62

6. On the Trail 78

7. "This Is the Place!" 93

8. Trouble Across the River 109

9. A Boy for a Man's Job 125

10. Monsieur Maxent Sees the Light . . 149

11. St. Louis, U. S. A. 170

Afterword 177

A Boy for
a Man's Job

CHAPTER 1

"A Boy Should Be Beaten!"

ONE more word from you, Auguste, and you leave the table. It is not for small boys to interrupt when their elders are talking!"

Papa Pierre spoke very sternly. Mamma sighed, and the younger children looked fearfully at Auguste. What had got into him tonight? Their big brother was supposed to be an example of good manners. Mamma was always saying so. "Why can't you be quiet and polite like Auguste?" "Auguste does not chatter." "Auguste does not interrupt." "Auguste is the only gentleman among you."

So it always was. But tonight, of all nights,

Auguste was forgetting his manners. And forgetting them before an honored guest!

Monsieur Maxent, their father's friend, sat at table, frowning heavily. Monsieur Maxent was a bachelor, with no patience for children. Mamma had warned them all before dinner that they must be very, very good. They had been good, eating their soup without a word or even a giggle.

Only Auguste had not been good. He had listened to Papa's talk with Monsieur Maxent. More than once he had put in a word. Mamma had shaken her head at him. His brother had stepped on his toes under the table. It was no use. For the third time Auguste interrupted. This time Papa spoke more sharply than he ever spoke to his children.

"I'm sorry, Papa Pierre," Auguste said now. But Monsieur Maxent was not satisfied.

"The boy should be beaten," the visitor said. "That's your trouble, Laclede. You spoil this stepson of yours with kindness. A good sound beating every day will improve his manners. Nothing else will do it."

"Usually Auguste's manners are very good,"

Pierre Laclede said mildly. "He forgets himself tonight because he is so interested in our expedition. Can you blame him? To a boy of his age it sounds like a most exciting adventure."

"Adventure!" the visitor snorted. "So that is what he thinks! Well, I will soon set him right on that."

He turned to Auguste, now eating with downcast eyes.

"Listen to me, young fellow!" Maxent's harsh voice made them all jump. "You think your father and I are planning an adventure, do you? Nothing of the sort. The king of France has given me permission to trade with the Indians along the upper Mississippi. I need a trading post to which the savages may bring their furs. Your stepfather knows the river and the Indians. I have offered him a partnership. He will go up the river and build the trading post. I will look after the office and warehouse here in New Orleans. From here we will ship the furs to France. If all goes well, our firm will prosper.

"There, now you see what it is, young **man**.

No adventure at all. Just a simple matter of business. Do you understand that now?"

"Yes, sir, and thank you for explaining it to me," Auguste said. "I think you are wise to stay here and let Papa Pierre go up the river, Monsieur Maxent. The wilderness is hard on old people. And it would be hard for you to fit into a dugout canoe, too. They are so very narrow, and you are so very wide, sir. But—"

Monsieur Maxent had just raised his wine-

glass to his lips. He set it down so hard that the wine splashed the white tablecloth. For a long moment no one spoke. Then the guest turned to the mother.

"Madame," he said furiously, "you will oblige me by removing your children from this room. At once, Madame. At once!"

Long after the younger children were asleep, Auguste was awake, waiting. Mamma had gone to her room. Downstairs he could hear the two men talking. Monsieur Maxent sounded calmer now. They were discussing the business they hoped would come from the new venture.

At last the front door closed. Then came Papa Pierre's light step on the stairs. He came into the room, carrying a candle. In his other hand was a small riding whip.

"Are you awake, my son?" Pierre Laclede spoke quietly so as not to disturb the other children.

Auguste approached his father.

"I'm awake, Papa Pierre. I'm waiting to tell you how sorry I am. I didn't mean to make Monsieur Maxent angry. I was trying to be polite. I was just about to say what a good business man he was. He got angry before I was through. Monsieur Maxent is an awfully hot-tempered man, isn't he, Papa Pierre? He gets angry over nothing."

"And is it nothing to tell a gentleman he is old and fat?" Laclede demanded.

"Did I say that? Oh, Papa, I didn't mean it that way! I told him he was wise. You heard me, Papa Pierre. It's very wise for a fat old gentleman to stay in the office here. He'll get a good price for the furs too. Honestly, Papa Pierre, I was trying to pay him a compliment. I thought he'd be pleased."

"Well, he was not pleased," Pierre Laclede said grimly. "I believe you, Auguste. I don't think you meant to insult our guest. You did insult him, however. You must be punished."

"Yes, Papa." He looked at the whip in his father's hand. Laclede's kind, gentle face was sad. "Monsieur Maxent said you must beat me, didn't he?" Auguste went on. "You never beat your children, Papa. Everyone knows that. But now you have to beat me, because Monsieur Maxent says so. Do you have to do what Monsieur Maxent says, then? I don't understand that."

Pierre Laclede sat down on the side of the bed.

"Listen, Auguste. You're a big boy now. You're old enough to understand how it is with us, my son."

He waited a minute, and then went on earnestly:

"I'm a poor man, Auguste. Ten years ago I came from France to New Orleans. I hoped to make my fortune in the New World. I began fur trading in a small way. I would go up the river with a few trinkets and buy a few skins from the Indians. When I came back to New Orleans, I would sell them to Monsieur Maxent at his big warehouse. It was a poor living, but enough for a single man.

"Then I met your mother. She was alone in the world with you, her little son. She had suffered much. My only thought has been to make her happy. It takes money to keep a family, Auguste. I have worked hard, but you know how poor we have been.

"And now comes my big chance. Monsieur

Maxent is a rich, important man. The king has given him the right to buy all the furs the Indians will sell. No one else has that right. It will mean a big business. Much money will be made."

"But Monsieur Maxent is already rich," Auguste put in. "Why do you have to help him get richer?"

Laclede smiled. "Because I wish to help myself, Auguste. Monsieur Maxent has chosen me for his partner. He might have had any trader in New Orleans, but he chose me. I shall make money too, my boy. Enough money to build a nice house for Mamma and the little ones. Enough money to send you all to a better school. Now do you see why I wish to please Monsieur Maxent?"

Auguste sighed. "I see, Papa. And I made him angry in your house. Does he blame you? Does he say you can't be his partner because I insulted him? Won't he let you go up the river now?"

"Oh, no, it's not so bad as that!" Laclede answered with a smile. "Monsieur Maxent thinks I am a bad father, but he knows I am

a good trader. Tomorrow I begin getting ready for the expedition. But tonight—" he stopped, and looked sadly at the boy.

"Tonight you must beat me," Auguste said bravely. "Is that all? I was afraid I'd spoiled everything for you. Why, this is nothing. Go on, Papa. Beat me. I'm ready."

Pierre Laclede raised his riding whip and brought it lightly down across the boy's shoulders. Once and once again the soft blow fell. Then the father threw the whip to the floor. The two looked at each other and laughed together.

"Well, that's over," Auguste said cheerfully. "You can tell Monsieur you did beat me, as he wished. Now I want to hear about the expedition, Papa. It's the most exciting thing that has ever happened. When do you start? What will you take with you? I had a million questions to ask, but Monsieur Maxent wouldn't let me talk. Do tell me all about it now."

They talked for a long time. Pierre Laclede had made many canoe trips up the great Mississippi. He knew the river well. He had friends among the Indians along the banks. The red men knew that he would give them a fair price for their furs. Monsieur Maxent had chosen well when he chose Laclede to lead this great expedition.

It would be very different from his other trips, he explained to Auguste. This time he was to build a town. First of all he would have to find the right place for it. The spot must be as far up the river as possible. It must be in good trapping country. Then, when the place was decided upon, work could begin.

"You'll need carpenters and stonemasons," Auguste said. "And you'll have to take along nails and hammers and things like that, won't you? And some big boats to carry them. Will Monsieur Maxent pay for those?"

Pierre Laclede nodded. "He will pay for everything. He puts his money into our partnership. I put in my time, and my knowledge of the country."

"And you do all the work," Auguste said. "But of course you have all the fun too. How can Monsieur Maxent bear to stay behind? It *is* an adventure, whatever he says. To build a town where nothing was before! I never heard of one man doing that. I thought towns just grew up, little by little, as more people came to live in them. I didn't know you could build one all at once. What shall you call your town, Papa? Lacledeville, after yourself? You should, because it will be your town. But I suppose that fussy old Monsieur Maxent will want it called after *him*."

Papa Pierre laughed. "We'll cross that bridge when we come to it, my son. There is everything to do before we worry about a name. Monsieur Maxent only got the king's letter today. It will take weeks to get ready. Tomorrow I must begin looking about for boats. Then I must find some strong, able men to form our company. I can't have any weaklings. There is hard work to be done. It won't be easy to find the sort of men I want."

Auguste studied his stepfather's face, and then spoke timidly.

"Papa Pierre, would you—would you think of taking me? Oh, I know I'm only thirteen," he went on quickly. "But I'm strong, and big for my age. I can paddle, and I shoot pretty well. It's true I don't know anything about building houses, but I can learn. And I wouldn't want any wages," he urged. "I'd pay to go, if I had any money! Oh, Papa Pierre, please, please take me! I'll work hard; I'll do everything you tell me! May I go?"

"And what would Mamma say to this?"

"She'd say yes, if you wanted it," Auguste answered. "We could have fun, Papa Pierre. You know we always have fun together. You said yourself you'd rather go fishing with me than with any man you know. Well, this is like a fishing trip, only bigger and better. Don't you *want* me with you, Papa Pierre?"

"I'd have to think about it," Laclede said slowly. "This is a serious business, Auguste. It is not a pleasure trip."

"I know, I know! But you said yourself I'm a big boy now. I'll be fourteen in two more months. I'm not so strong as a man. Maybe I couldn't do all the work a man can do. But surely there'd be some jobs for a boy on such a trip. There are always two or three boys on the ships that come from France. Once I heard a sea captain say that a willing, active boy more than earned his passage. I think I could earn my passage on your expedition, Papa Pierre."

"Well—" Laclede hesitated, and Auguste could see he was almost persuaded. "But how about school?" was the next question. Auguste was ready for that one.

"School vacation begins in two weeks," he

said eagerly. "You won't be ready to start before then. And you know this is my last term with Master Lamar. Then I'll be ready for the Academy."

Laclede sighed. The Academy, as he and Auguste both knew, cost more than the family could now afford. If the expedition succeeded, there would be money for Auguste's schooling. The profits would not come until spring. Whatever happened, there would be no school for Auguste this winter.

Auguste reminded him of this now. "So you see, Papa Pierre, I wouldn't be missing school by going with you. There is no reason why you shouldn't take me. Unless you really don't want me. *Don't* you want me with you, Papa Pierre?"

The big man looked thoughtfully down into the eager face. It was true that young Auguste was a good companion on a fishing trip. He never complained of cold or wet, or smoking fires and scanty food. The boy always had a cheerful laugh and a joke, no matter how uncomfortable he might be. There would be discomfort in plenty on this expedition. Yes, it would be pleasant to have this laughing, happy boy along.

"I do want you, my son," he said at last. "If your mother consents—"

"She will, she will!" In his excitement Auguste forgot to keep his voice low. In the far corner his baby brother stirred and whimpered. Laclede shook his head at Auguste.

"Mamma will be in to scold us both," he whispered. "Good night, my boy. Tomorrow we will see about it."

CHAPTER 2

"You Are Not to Go"

IT took nearly a month to get the expedition ready. Monsieur Maxent supplied two boats of the kind the French called bateaux. A bateau was a flat-bottomed barge, sometimes very small, sometimes large enough to hold twenty tons of cargo. Monsieur Maxent's boats were of the largest size. Besides the two big barges, there were several Indian canoes.

Auguste watched the loading. From Monsieur Maxent's warehouse came bolts of bright calico, barrels and bottles of rum, brandy and wine, big boxes of knives and beads and fishhooks. One day the boy heard the two partners talking.

16

"You are giving us more trade goods than we need, sir," Laclede said. "This is not a trading expedition. In the beginning we must build the town. When that is done, then trade can begin. But on this trip it is more important to take things the town needs. I would like machinery to set up a mill. We can get grain from the Indians and grind it there. I want to take some plows. Our men can begin to start their own little farms. When their wives come, their homes will be waiting for them."

"Their wives? What nonsense is this?" Monsieur Maxent scowled. "I send you to build a trading post. We will need docks for boats to land. We will need a good warehouse where our goods can be stored. There must be stout walls to keep the thieving savages out. That is all. What is this talk of women and homes?"

Laclede smiled. "I see it differently, sir. I see a real town, where people live and bring up their children. If I have my way, I shall take only married men with me. As soon as houses are built, they will come back for their families. Don't you see, Monsieur Maxent?"

His voice was very earnest. "We have a chance that is not given to many men. A trading post, what is that? We have a chance to build a *city!* I hope—"

"I will not listen to such foolishness!" the old man interrupted. "A city in the wilderness, among savages! I thought you were a man of sense, Laclede. You talk like a child. You make no more sense than—than this simple-minded boy of yours, always at our heels!" He turned his frown upon young Auguste. "Get home to your mammy, child! I find you a nuisance."

"Yes, sir." Auguste bowed politely, as he had been taught to do, and hurried away.

After that he tried to keep out of Monsieur Maxent's sight. But whenever the old man was safely in his office, Auguste followed Laclede about his preparations. The boy was the first to know his stepfather's great worry. Laclede was having a hard time hiring good men for the expedition.

"It's the wages," he explained to Auguste. "Monsieur Maxent is spending a great deal of money on boats and trade goods. He says we must save somewhere. He thinks the place to save is on wages. For what he offers, I cannot get the men I want. I need carpenters, stone-masons, skilled workmen. Why should they come for less pay than they can get here in New Orleans? That is what they ask me. And I have no answer."

"But so many men come to be hired," Auguste said. "They crowd our doorstep every morning."

"Yes, but such men! Young fools who are tired of their homes. Gamblers in trouble with the police. Worthless loafers who don't know what an honest day's work means. What can I do with such riffraff? Yet what else can I have on the pay Maxent offers? If I could only make him see . . .!"

They were walking home after a long day on the docks. Auguste looked up into his step-father's face and smiled.

"Anyway, you'll have me, Papa Pierre. That's one you can depend on, at least."

Pierre Laclede stopped short. He hesitated a minute, looking away toward the river. Then he said quietly, "I'm afraid not,

Auguste. I've been dreading to tell you this. You must take it like a man, my son. You are not to go."

"Not go? Papa, you can't mean that! Why, it's been settled from the very beginning. That first night, don't you remember? You said if Mamma consents. And she did consent. I asked her the very next day. Papa, you *promised!*"

"I know, my son. *I* promised. Monsieur Maxent did not. I'm sorry. I can't tell you how sorry I am. But there it is. I cannot take you."

"*He* said so?"

"Yes, Auguste. I didn't want to tell you until I was sure. I have spoken to him more than once, hoping he would change his mind. He will not change it. And it is his expedition. He has the say."

"But why, Papa Pierre? Is it—is it because I was rude to him that night? Oh, why didn't I bite off my tongue before I called him old and fat!"

"Don't blame yourself, my son. It was not that alone. Monsieur Maxent simply has no use for children. He thinks their place is with their mothers. He says you'd cry, or get sick, or . . ."

"But I'm nearly fourteen!" Auguste broke in. "Does he think I'm a baby? I never heard such nonsense. Oh, this Monsieur Maxent is a hard, cruel man, Papa!"

Laclede shook his head. "No, Auguste. Maxent is hard, maybe. He is not cruel. He is a merchant, thinking first and always of his

profits. If he believed that you would be useful, he would not object to your going. He
does not think so, and I cannot make him see
it. I've done all I can. I know this is a blow to
you, Auguste. You must take it like the brave
boy you are."

They walked on in silence. Auguste felt
tears gathering in his eyes, but he blinked
them back. Monsieur Maxent had said he
would cry. Well, he would not cry. Not now,
and not when the boats pushed off without
him. He would show them all that he was not
a baby. But his heart was very heavy as he
looked back at the loaded boats. Soon, very
soon they would move up the river. They
would pass the bend he knew. They would go
on and on, into the land he had never seen.
Adventure waited there, but not for him. He
blinked so hard that he stumbled, for he could
not see the path.

Three days later, on the third of August,
1763, the expedition left New Orleans. The
start was made at noon. Laclede had gathered
fifty men. Out of that number, only about ten

were the sober, skilled workmen he had hoped for.

The rest were a sorry lot, tramps and drunkards and petty criminals. They were the best that Laclede could find for the wages he was able to offer. He had tried to pick the strongest and hardiest ones. The labor of getting the barges upstream would be enormous. He could only hope that these men would be equal to it.

The Laclede family came down to see the departure. Monsieur Maxent was there too, bustling about, giving orders and fussing over the cargo. He arrived in his handsome carriage, driven by a young Indian boy. After Maxent got out, the driver tied the horses and came to stand respectfully near the Lacledes. Auguste turned and smiled at him.

"Good morning, Charlie."

"Good morning, Master Auguste." The driver looked at Auguste's clothes, the Sunday suit he had put on for the occasion. "You do not go with your father, then?"

Monsieur Maxent was approaching Madame Laclede and the children. Auguste dropped back to where the other boy stood.

Charlie Half-and-Half, as he was called, was an old friend. He was an orphan, half-white, half-Indian, with no family and no home. Ever since Auguste could remember he had worked at odd jobs around the Maxent warehouse. He was two years older than Auguste, but smaller, and very thin. Charlie had taught Auguste to swim and to paddle a canoe.

That had been long ago, when both boys were much younger. Auguste saw little of Charlie nowadays. Auguste himself was in school. Monsieur Maxent kept Charlie busy, now that he was old enough to do a man's work. Madame Laclede, who liked the boy, thought he was overworked. He looked after the horses, waited at table, helped in the warehouse and on the dock. All this for a bed in the stable, for meals and worn-out clothing.

Charlie looked at Auguste now with sympathy in his soft brown eyes. They were not Indian eyes, black and piercing, but a clear golden brown. From his Indian mother Charlie had high cheekbones and a bronze skin, but his eyes and his dark brown, slightly curling hair recalled a white man's.

"You wanted to go, didn't you?" Charlie said now. "I know how you feel. I wanted to go too. But Monsieur Maxent said no."

"I wanted it more than anything on earth! And Papa Pierre would have taken me too." Auguste stopped and looked at his friend. "*You* wanted to go? Oh, Charlie, if we only could! Both of us, together, wouldn't it be wonderful? And only that hateful, stingy old man—"

"Hush, Master Auguste, hush!" Charlie spoke too late. Monsieur Maxent turned around and glared at the two boys. He could not have heard the words, but their chatter annoyed him.

"Get back to your horses, Charlie," he said harshly.

"Yes, Master." The boy bowed and slipped away. Auguste looked after him, a frown gathering on his face. Auguste always frowned when he was thinking hard.

And now came the blare of music as the town band marched down the street. Pierre Laclede was to be seen off in style. Monsieur Maxent had provided for that.

Laclede's company stood at attention, fifty stalwart men, dressed in woodsmen's buckskin clothing. They stood stiffly in the hot sun while the mayor of New Orleans made a long speech. Monsieur Maxent, very fine in his satin and ruffles, followed it with a longer one. Father Marcy from the cathedral asked a blessing on the expedition. Then came a burst of

music, and the French flag was run up to the masthead of the leading barge.

Auguste Chouteau had heard not a word of the speeches or the prayers. He was deaf to the stirring music. He stood quietly through it all, thinking so hard that his head ached. Then, as the men began to cast off the ropes, his frown vanished. Quietly he moved toward the spot where Charlie stood beside Monsieur Maxent's carriage. He spoke softly under cover of the rolling drums.

"Look, Charlie. Meet me here as soon as it's dark. This is important! You'll come?"

The Indian boy nodded. Auguste hurried back to take his place with his brothers and sister. The music died away. Laclede shook hands with all the gentlemen. Then he kissed his wife and children and stepped aboard the first barge. The men took their places. The band struck up a lively march. Slowly, creakingly, the loaded boats got under way. Pierre Laclede was off to found his city.

Home again, Mamma looked anxiously at Auguste as he took his place at table. Her gentle heart ached for the boy, so bitterly disappointed in all he had hoped for. Madame Laclede, who knew how her son liked to make himself useful, thought Monsieur Maxent had been very foolish. Auguste would have been worth more to the expedition than any of the grown men. She knew that was her husband's opinion too. Pierre Laclede was as disappointed as the boy himself. Well, there was nothing to be done about it now. She hoped Auguste would not be too unhappy.

With relief the mother saw that her son ate a hearty supper. He talked cheerfully with her and the children. But when she sent the little ones up to bed, he went with them. Once in the attic bedroom, he took his slate over to the window.

"Are you studying tonight, brother?" little Pierre asked.

Auguste nodded. "I have some writing to do. I won't disturb you. Go to sleep."

He sat long by the fading daylight, writing and rubbing out and writing again. At last he was satisfied. He propped the slate on his pillow. His mother would see it in the morning.

If Monsieur Maxent came asking questions, Mamma could tell him she had known nothing until it was too late. Dear Mamma, she would be glad. She wanted him to be with Papa Pierre.

It was nearly dark now. The other children were sound asleep. Moving quietly, Auguste changed into his everyday clothes. Into his pocket went the little silver snuffbox that had been his grandfather's. It was his very own, Mamma had given it to him when he had the measles, to keep his pills in. Then he made up a small bundle. An extra shirt and stockings, his knife, and his rosary—what else would he need? From a drawer he took his St. Christopher medal. St. Christopher, patron saint of travelers—that he would certainly need!

With the bundle over his shoulder, he went to the head of the stair and listened. His mother was in the kitchen, setting tomorrow's bread. He slipped silently down the stairs. At the door he stood a minute. His fingers touched the St. Christopher medal around his neck. His lips moved in silent prayer. Then, throwing a kiss toward the kitchen, he ran swiftly down the street.

Charlie Half-and-Half was waiting on the empty dock. Auguste wasted no time.

"Charlie, you have a canoe. Go bring it around."

The Indian boy peered at him in the gathering darkness. "Monsieur Maxent's canoe, do you mean? The one I use to catch fish for the table?"

"Yes, that one. Bring extra paddles, too. And—here." He took the silver snuffbox from his pocket. "Leave this on your bed, where Monsieur Maxent can find it. It will pay for the canoe. Now hurry!"

"But Master Auguste, I don't understand. It's much too late for fishing tonight. Besides, I haven't Monsieur Maxent's permission. If you want fish—"

"Fish, fish! Who said anything about fish? It isn't for fishing that we'll need the canoe— although I expect we'll do some before we're through. Now hurry, Charlie!"

"Not fishing? Then where are we going, Master Auguste?"

"Where do you think? Where do we want to go? Both of us? We're going where Monsieur Maxent can't give us orders any more. Don't stand there staring, Charlie. We're going up the Mississippi!"

CHAPTER 3

Alone on the River

THE boys paddled carefully out of the harbor, keeping away from the ships. Behind them, the lights and sounds of the town slowly faded. The little French city of New Orleans was a gay place, fond of music and dancing. The strains of a fiddle came faintly across the water, and the sound of laughter. But soon they rounded a bend and left it all behind them. They were alone on the dark river, with only the stars for company.

They had hardly dared to speak until they were free of the town. When the last light faded behind them, Auguste drew a long breath.

"Well, we made it, Charlie. Monsieur Maxent can't stop us now. I wish I could see his face when he finds us gone!"

"He will be angry." The Indian boy's voice was calm. "I think he will send word to Monsieur Laclede that I must come back. And if I come, he will have me beaten."

"But you won't come," Auguste said eagerly. "Why should you? You're not his slave. It's true that he's given you food and shelter. But you have earned all he has given you. Any other master would have paid you wages besides. You don't owe Monsieur Maxent anything, Charlie."

"I have thought that too," Charlie answered. "I did not ask to work for him. One of the Maxent traders brought me down the river in the first place. I can just remember it. I must have been about five or six. I had never left my Indian village before."

"Did the trader steal you?" Auguste asked.

"Oh, no. This is how it was. I lived in a small village on the bank of the Mississippi. I do not know the name of our tribe. I was so young, you see. But I know there was a big fight with another tribe. They killed all my people and burned the huts. My mother, my grandfather—all were killed. The traders saw the smoke from the river. It was all over when they came. They found me crouching in the bushes, half-mad with terror. I was the only living thing in the ruined village."

"How terrible! Was your father killed too?" Auguste asked.

"He was not there. He was away, fighting the British. My father is a soldier of the French king," Charlie said proudly. "Or perhaps I should say he *was* a soldier. I do not know if he still lives. I cannot remember him at all. I know only what my mother told me. And she is dead."

Charlie sighed, and was silent. The two boys paddled on. It was growing lighter now, as a full moon slowly rose into the night sky. Soon the muddy river turned into a sheet of silver.

The moonlight was welcome, for it showed them the sandbars and sunken tree trunks they must avoid. There were no other boats on the river. There was no sound but the lapping water and sometimes the distant cry of a night bird.

Although the summer night was warm, Auguste shivered a little.

"It's lonely out here," he said. "I feel as if we were the only people in the world. I'll be glad when we catch up with Papa Pierre and the others."

"It should not be long," Charlie said cheerfully. "Their heavy boats are very slow. And they would not travel at night. We will catch them at their first camp."

"I hope so." Auguste moved his aching knees. Both boys were kneeling on the floor of the canoe. Charlie was in front, his keen eyes finding their course over the moonlit water. The Indian boy's arms rose and fell steadily. He seemed never to tire. But Auguste was beginning to ache all over. His paddle seemed so heavy he could scarcely lift it.

And so the long night wore on. As the hours passed, the boys spoke very little. They were going against the river current, which seemed to get stronger all the time. Even Charlie's stroke slowed a little. Auguste, kneeling be-

hind him, was fighting off sleep. He thought
with longing of his comfortable attic bed. If
only he could throw his aching bones down
upon it, and sleep, and sleep . . .

"Master Auguste!" Charlie spoke sharply,
and Auguste started broad awake. The scene
had changed. Thick clouds covered the sky.

The air was chill. Rain was beginning to fall. It was so dark now that Auguste could scarcely see his companion.

"We can't go on," Charlie said. "We'll have to pull into the bank until daylight. Come now, Master Auguste. Rouse yourself. This will not be easy."

Slowly, carefully, Charlie edged the canoe toward the nearer shore. They just missed the jagged fork of an old log lodged in a sandbar. It could have split their frail canoe and ended their voyage then and there.

Auguste could see only blackness ahead of them. But the Indian boy's sharper eyes caught the welcome bushes. He dropped his paddle and grabbed the tough branches. He pulled hard on them, and the canoe slid into the muddy bank.

They piled out into the drenching rain. There was no shelter.

"We'll turn the canoe over and get under it," Charlie said. "That is all we can do until daylight comes."

It was cramped and uncomfortable under the canoe, but at least they were out of the rain. They sat hunched in the mud, stiff and aching, and very cold. There was no room to stretch out. The canoe rested on their shoulders. They had to bend their heads down to their knees.

"It's funny," Auguste said through chattering teeth. "In the canoe I was so sleepy I couldn't keep my eyes open. Now I'm wide-awake. Are you sleepy, Charlie?"

"Sleepy? No. I am cold. And also I am hungry. I had no supper tonight. When I had served my master his meal, I left to meet you. There was no time to wait for the scraps the cook would have given me."

"Is that what you had to eat—the scraps from the table?" Auguste spoke indignantly. "No wonder you're so thin, Charlie."

"Many an orphan has less," the Indian boy reminded him. "So Monsieur Maxent often told me. I do not complain. There are very good scraps at Monsieur Maxent's house. His cook sets a fine table."

"Yes, a fine table for *him!* Anyone would know that by looking at his fat stomach. Well, I wish you hadn't begun to talk about food,

Charlie. Now I'm hungry too. But I suppose there's nothing we can do about it."

"There is nothing, so we will not think of it any more," Charlie said cheerfully. "When we find Monsieur Pierre, then we will eat. Try now to sleep a little, Master Auguste. It will make the night go faster."

The rain drummed down upon the canoe. Huddled together, the two boys dozed. This time Auguste was the first to wake. The rain had stopped. A cold gray light crept under the canoe. The dawn had come.

As Auguste moved beside him, the Indian boy opened his eyes. "Morning, at last? Good. Then we can get on."

They pushed the canoe aside and stood up. Auguste gave a little cry of pain.

"You are stiff, Master Auguste?" Charlie said. "That is to be expected. Your muscles are not used to such a long stretch of paddling. And your hands—yes, I see. They are blistered. I am sorry."

"Oh, I'm all right." Auguste stretched and began to jump around. "It's better after I've moved my arms and legs a little. My hands will soon toughen up. Well, let's go. No use waiting for breakfast here."

They launched the canoe and set off. The sun had not yet risen. Mist hung low over the river. The first few minutes of paddling were painful for both of them. It took a long time to get the canoe around the next bend. When they did, Charlie gave a delighted shout.

"There they are, Master Auguste! See, far ahead. There is the campfire. And I can just make out the boats."

The light was stronger now. The mist was thinning. Through it, far up the stream, Auguste could make out a low bluff. At its foot was the red gleam of fire. Then the mist closed in again and hid everything.

"Hurry, Master Auguste," Charlie urged. "They'll be breaking camp any minute now. We must reach them before they have eaten all the breakfast."

All Auguste's pain seemed to vanish. He felt fine and strong and happy.

"Let's shout to tell them we're coming. No, better still, let's sing. I feel like singing, Charlie. Come on, now, as loud as you can!"

Pierre Laclede, just finishing breakfast by the fire, jumped to his feet. Auguste's favorite song! Surely, surely it could not be—

But it was. Faint at first, then growing stronger, the gay words floated nearer on the morning air.

"Three ducks came swimming to our pond,
Fal lal la la la,
Our neighbor claims that they are his,
The pond is ours, the ducks are ours,
Fal lal la la la.
Tonight we eat roast duck, Fal la,
Tonight we eat roast duck!"

The sun's first rays struck the yellow water, turning it to dazzling gold. On that golden sea a tiny canoe bobbed merrily toward the camp.

Pierre Laclede turned to one of his men. "Don't put out the fire yet, Émile. And put the soup pot back on. There will be a slight delay in starting. My son is joining us."

The two boys, filled with soup and bread, had told their story. They waited now for Laclede to speak. Would he send them home again? Would he let them go on with the party? Auguste held his breath.

"Monsieur Maxent will not be pleased," Laclede said at last. "He does not understand how useful an active boy can be on the river. For my part, I am glad to have you both. I will not send you back. If you work well, I can make things right with my partner. If you do not—well, then I must take the blame."

"There won't be any blame, Papa Pierre," Auguste said eagerly. "Charlie and I will work—oh, you'll see how hard! You won't be sorry you let us stay."

"I hope not." Laclede spoke sternly, but there was a twinkle in his eye. Safely away from New Orleans, he did not worry too much about Monsieur Maxent's wishes. In the city, the rich merchant was the boss; but here on the river Laclede took command. In his opinion, Maxent had already meddled too much in the choice of men. He was too far away to meddle now.

The men were rolling their blankets and getting ready to move on. The open barges had no sleeping quarters. All the space was taken up by the barrels and crates of supplies. Throughout the trip the party would sleep on shore, under the open sky.

"What shall we do, Papa Pierre?" Auguste
asked. "Give us a job. We want to show you
how we can work."

Laclede smiled. "Don't worry, I'll find
plenty of work for you. This morning I think
you'd better rest. Tie your canoe behind one

of the barges. Then lie down among the barrels and get some sleep. Here are some blankets."

"But Papa, we are here to work!"

"You are here to obey my orders," the big man answered. "You are both worn out from your hard night. You're no good to me until you have rested. I order you to rest."

He turned away. The two boys made their canoe fast and then climbed aboard the nearest barge. How good it felt to snuggle down in a nest of blankets, under the warm sun! They had not known how tired they were. Both boys were asleep before the boat began to move.

It was late afternoon when Auguste awoke. Everything was strangely quiet. He sat up and looked around him. Except for Charlie sleeping beside him, he was alone on the barge. The other big boat had disappeared. There was no sign of the canoes or their paddlers.

Auguste shook his friend. "Charlie, wake up! Something dreadful has happened. They're all gone. We're alone again!"

The Indian boy sat up and rubbed his eyes. Then he laughed.

"They haven't gone far. Look up, Master Auguste. Right above your head. There, do you see the rope leading from the mast? The men are ashore, cutting a towpath. Listen. You can hear them chopping."

The shore was very close. It was covered with a low growth of trees. The branches kept them from seeing anyone. But listening now, Auguste could hear the sound of axes, and of men's voices. He looked up and saw the tall pole just above him. From it a long rope hung slack, its end disappearing into the clump of trees. Their barge was not moving.

"Oh, they're using the cordelle!" Auguste exclaimed excitedly. "This I have never seen. The barges were poled out of the harbor. But Papa Pierre did say he'd use the cordelle when he got into the open river. I couldn't figure out how it worked."

"It is very simple, Master Auguste. The rope is fastened to the mast. The men walk along the bank, pulling on the rope. So the boat moves through the water. In many places there is a good towpath where others have tramped it down. Here, it seems, there is none.

So our men must stop to cut a path through
the trees. I think they have finished now. Yes,
we are beginning to move."

"I wonder what time it is? I hope it won't
be too long until we make camp. I'm hungry
again."

"We have not earned our food today, Master Auguste. But perhaps Monsieur Pierre
will find work for us before we sleep. I shall
feel happier when I can begin to be useful to
him."

CHAPTER 4

The Boys Find Their Job

LOOKING back, Charlie and Auguste could see the other barge following at some distance. Each of the two barges had its team of fifteen men hauling on the towrope. The canoes hovered along the shore. Towing was hard work. When a man became too tired for it, he changed places with a man from one of the canoes.

Shading his eyes from the sun, Auguste peered down the river.

"I can't see Papa Pierre anywhere, Charlie. I wonder where he is."

"His canoe is not among those, Master Auguste. Perhaps he has gone on ahead to

48

find a stopping place for the night. The sun is getting low."

Charlie's guess was correct. A little later they saw Pierre Laclede coming toward them from upriver. The other canoes were all clumsy dugouts made of hollowed logs. Laclede had a swift little birch-bark canoe, brought down from the North. With it he could dart up and down the river, covering miles while the heavy barges crept along. In this way he could keep his eye on everything, as a leader should.

He came alongside the barge now and greeted the boys cheerfully.

"You have had a long sleep? That is good. I've found a fine spot for us up ahead. I wonder if you wouldn't like to go on now and get a fire going? I've marked some trees so you'll know the place."

Willingly the boys ran to their canoe. Laclede made sure they had flint and tinder for fire. Then they pushed off and soon left the barge behind.

The camping place was far better than the one of the previous night. A little spring bubbled out of clean sand. There was a stretch of tall green grass. In no time the boys had gathered dead wood and built a fire. Then Charlie Half-and-Half took out his knife.

"You have your knife too, Master Auguste?" he asked. "Then come into the woods. We will cut some green branches for sleeping. The men will be tired. They will be glad to find their beds waiting."

They cut armload after armload of leafy branches, piling them high in the clearing. They were still busy with this when the first men came in, pulling the towrope of the leading barge. The rope was looped around the tree, there was a series of mighty pulls, and the barge bumped against the bank. The other big boat soon followed, and then the canoes with their men.

Auguste had been wondering just what there would be for supper. He knew that there was bread on the barges—great stacks of crusty French loaves. But bread alone made a poor meal for hungry men. And he and Charlie had scraped the soup pot clean at breakfast time.

He was relieved to see the men from the

canoes lift out long strings of fish. They had not been idle while they waited their turn on the towrope. As soon as the canoe men arrived they began cleaning the fish.

Laclede, who came last, leaped lightly ashore.

"A good catch, men," he said. "Now let's see—the frying pans would be in the last barge. And a can of olive oil. Will you get them, Charlie? Auguste, you open a bag of corn meal. We'll soon have our supper now."

The oil and the corn meal were trampled into the ground as the men crowded around, each trying to prepare the fish he had snatched for himself. There was still more confusion over the frying pans. Everyone was in a hurry. No one wanted to wait his turn. Voices rose angrily. There were loud oaths and a blow or two.

At last Laclede raised his voice in a shout.

"Men! Listen to me. This will not do. We must have order. There are six frying pans here. I will appoint six cooks. Jean, Pierre, Emile—and you three over there. You are the cooks. Every man will give his fish to you. You will cook them as speedily as may be. You others will sit down and wait quietly. Let me hear no more grumbling."

There was grumbling in plenty as the men sullenly gave up their fish and sat down on the grass. Charlie Half-and-Half slipped quietly up to Laclede.

"The bread, Monsieur Pierre—may we give them their bread now? They will be more patient if they have something to munch while they wait."

"A good idea, Charlie. Auguste, help him give out the bread."

Laclede sat down and leaned wearily against a tree. He had made many expeditions before, but never with more than three or four companions. Fifty men—this was different! There would have to be new ways of doing things. How could fifty men be fed every day, in peace and order?

This was only the last difficulty of a difficult day. The men had not taken kindly to the hard work of towing. There had been quarrels, complaints, and a maddening slowness. At this rate, it would be months before they would

reach where they were going. Laclede sighed
and closed his eyes. For him, too, this first day
had been a hard one.

"Your supper, Monsieur Pierre." Laclede
opened his eyes. There was a delicious smell
of broiled fish. Charlie was holding a plate under his nose—three river catfish, split and bub-
bling brown, and thick slices of white bread.

"Eat while it is hot, sir," the Indian boy urged. "It will restore your strength."

Laclede straightened and looked about him. Some of the men were eating. Others were still waiting, while the cooks jostled one another around the fire.

"The men must be fed first," the leader said. "You should not have used a frying pan for me, Charlie."

The Indian boy laughed.

"Frying pan, what is that? A good fish needs no pan. Master Auguste and I built a little fire of our own. Over it we cooked your fish. We spitted it on a stick, as my people do. That is better than any pan. Taste it and you will see."

While he spoke, Auguste left his fire and came toward them. He was carrying a platter of fish and bread.

"May we eat our supper with you, Papa Pierre?"

"Sit down, boys. You have done well. I have never seen fish better cooked."

All three were hungry. They spoke little until the last crumb was gone. By that time the men, too, had had their suppers. They were pleased to find they need not cut branches for their beds. Each man carried an armful of boughs to a spot on the grass. He spread his blanket over the boughs and stretched out. Before long everyone was asleep except Laclede and the two boys.

"I'll make your bed wherever you say, Monsieur Pierre," Charlie offered. "Perhaps it should be at a little distance. There is a great deal of snoring here."

Laclede laughed. "Just as you say, Charlie. I am in your hands."

They found a good spot beyond a clump of bushes. The boys spread their own beds near the leader's.

"I expect you're too sleepy to talk, Papa Pierre," Auguste said. "I had something to ask you, but it can wait till morning."

"It need not wait. Speak now, boy. What is it?"

"It's about the camp," Auguste said earnestly. "Papa Pierre, we could manage better than we did tonight. But first I must ask you this. Do you plan for Charlie and me to take turns on the towrope?"

Laclede smiled. "I'm afraid you boys aren't strong enough for that. It's a job for grown men."

"We thought you would say that, Papa Pierre. Well, then, this is what we thought we could do. As the fish are caught, we could gather them from the other canoes. Then we could go ahead to the night camp. While the barges are coming up we could be cooking the fish. By the time the men would be in we'd have their supper ready. It would save all the trouble we had tonight. And I think the men would like it."

"I'm sure they would. But Auguste, this would be a big job for two boys. Cooking for fifty men! I really don't see how you could do it."

"We could do it, sir," Charlie Half-and-Half put in. "You saw how badly six cooks did tonight. Two good cooks are far better than six bad ones. I am a very good cook, sir. And Master Auguste is learning fast."

Auguste gave his friend a poke with his elbow.

"I told you not to call me that any more,

Charlie. There are no masters here on the river. You are my friend Charlie and I am your friend Auguste."

"Yes, Master—yes, my friend Auguste. Well, sir? Will you let us try?"

Laclede hesitated. "It won't always be fish to cook," he warned. "When the men have settled down to their jobs, I'll have time for some hunting. How are you at cooking deer meat and wild turkey, Charlie?"

The Indian boy smiled. "Bring me a deer or a turkey, sir, and you shall see."

"Well, I've always cooked for myself on these trips," Laclede said. "I'll admit that no fish of mine ever tasted like the fish you gave me tonight. If you boys want the cook's job, it's yours. But remember, if the work is too much for you, you must ask for help. And now let me get some sleep. Don't forget to say your prayers, Auguste."

"I won't forget, Papa."

But Auguste was not ready yet for his night-time prayer. The two boys lay long in the darkness, whispering together. They made great plans for their new job. They would show Monsieur Maxent that the expedition could not have done without them!

Supper the next night went very smoothly. The first men to arrive found their meal waiting for them. While they ate, the boys cooked for the second group, and then the third. The barges and canoes never came in together. There was always time to get ready for the next group.

Soon Laclede was able to spend some time in the woods with his hunting rifle. Often Auguste and Charlie went with him. Turkey and wild duck, venison and rabbit stew made a welcome change. Whatever their other complaints, the men could not complain of their food.

Their other complaints were many, however. As the long hot days dragged on, the men grew more sullen. Most of them had never worked so hard before. They began to think up excuses to leave the towrope. One afternoon Laclede found two men hiding among the barrels on one of the barges. They had spent the day in idleness, riding in comfort while their comrades towed them along.

At supper that night Laclede spoke severely to the men. There must be no shirking, he warned them. They were here to work. It was true that the work was hard. It was true that the sun was hot, that the mosquitoes and wood ticks were pests. Cutting a path through trees and thorny bushes was no fun. Of all this he had warned them in New Orleans. If they could not stand it, they should not have come.

"If we'd known what it was like, we wouldn't have come," one man said boldly. "Seems to me we're no better than horses, doing horses' work. And we get no more rum than a horse would get!" he ended angrily.

The man Émile had been a troublemaker from the start. Tonight Laclede lost patience with him.

"If I hear another complaint from you, Émile," he said sternly, "I'll cut off your rum entirely. Remember that now, and mind your manners. And the rest of you, remember what I have said. I'll have no shirking. Every man of you has work to do. I expect to see that you do it."

Muttering, the men went to their beds.

That night Auguste woke to hear voices and stealthy movements. Just some of the men getting a drink of water, he thought.

In the morning it was found that one of the canoes was missing. With it had gone Émile and two friends. Gone also was a small cask of rum from one of the barges.

Laclede took the desertion calmly. "They were no good to me. I'm glad to be rid of them. But from now on I shall put a guard over the canoes at night."

A guard was posted every night. Work on the towpath went faster, but the grumbling increased.

In spite of the grumbling, the expedition toiled on. Days went by, and weeks. In September Auguste had his fourteenth birthday. Summer turned into autumn. The nights were much colder now. Pierre Laclede began to look anxious. River travel would end with the coming of winter.

It was late October when they reached the first white settlement. It was the tiny French town of Ste. Geneviève.

CHAPTER 5

At Ste. Geneviève

KNOWING they were near the town, Laclede had gone ahead, taking the two
boys with him.

"We'll find friends here," he said, as they
approached the landing. "I've visited Ste.
Geneviève before, on my trading trips. If I'm
not mistaken, that's my old friend Monsieur
Vallé coming to meet us."

Vallé, a rosy-cheeked French farmer,
grasped Laclede's hand warmly.

"Welcome to Ste. Geneviève, Monsieur
Laclede. This is a pleasant surprise. You'll be
my guest, of course. And your companions—?"

"My son Auguste, and his friend Charles."

Laclede introduced the boys to Vallé and to the other townspeople who came forward.

There was a little talk, and then Monsieur Vallé said, "Come along to my house, Monsieur Laclede. You must be tired and hungry. My wife will scold if I keep you standing here after your long journey."

Laclede shook his head. "Not yet, Vallé. I must wait for the rest of my party. Later, I'll be glad to visit your home."

"There are more to come? Well, bring them along. My house is large."

Pierre Laclede laughed. "I have forty-seven men with me, my friend."

"Forty-seven? Well—" Vallé hesitated, and a man in the group spoke up.

"I can take three or four of them, Monsieur Laclede. And no doubt my neighbors have room for some."

The warm-hearted villagers were quick with their offers. It was soon arranged that the men would be well cared for.

The boats came in before dark. Laclede saw that his men were settled for the night. Vallé had gone ahead to warn his wife. When

Laclede and the two boys walked up to the house, supper was already on the table.

Two priests had joined the family for supper. One was Father Meurin, of the Ste. Geneviève church. With him was a younger man, Father Paul. The second priest had just come down from Quebec. He was to take charge of the church at Kaskaskia, across the river. The old priest there had fallen ill and had returned to France. Father Paul was staying in Ste. Geneviève until a house could be made ready for him.

"You have visited your new parish?" Laclede asked. "And how do you find Kaskaskia, Father Paul?"

The young priest sighed. "I find the people in great trouble, sir. They do not like the prospect of living under Protestant rule."

"Protestant?" Laclede looked surprised. "Since when has the French government turned Protestant? I do not understand you, Father."

"You have not heard, Laclede," Monsieur Vallé put in. "You have been long on the river. The war with England is over at last."

"I knew that," Laclede said. "It ended three years ago, when the enemy took Montreal."

"The fighting ended then," Vallé said. "But it is only now, this year, that the peace treaty has been signed. The treaty has brought great changes."

The war of which they spoke was the French and Indian War. It had been a bitter struggle between France and England over the possession of North America. The war had ended in defeat for the French.

This much Laclede already knew. Now, for the first time, he heard the terms of the treaty. France gave up to England all her land east of the Mississippi. The Illinois side of the river, with its scattered French settlements, was now English territory.

"And England is a Protestant country," he said, when Vallé had explained the treaty to him. "Now I understand, Father, why you say Kaskaskia is under Protestant rule. But surely the English will not interfere with the religion of our people."

"They have promised not to do that. But already they are bringing in English settlers.

Kaskaskia is filling up with men from Virginia and New England. Soon the French will be crowded out. Many families have already left."

"Some of them came here to Ste. Geneviève," Vallé put in. "Frenchmen will not live where they must be ruled by Englishmen."

"And this side of the river is still French? I see."

Laclede was silent for a while. This news made a difference to his plans. He had not yet decided on which side of the river to build his city. Now, it seemed, he had no choice. The east bank, in English hands, was closed to him. Well, this west bank would do well enough.

Vallé, hearing of Laclede's plan to found a city, urged him to look no farther. Here was Ste. Geneviève, on the river, on good farming land. There was a lead mine near. From the wilderness beyond it, the Indians brought their furs to trade. What more could anyone ask?

Laclede promised to think it over. In the morning he would have a good look around. It might be that he had reached the end of his journey.

The party spent a week in Ste. Geneviève. It was not a happy week. Laclede's men behaved very badly. With no work to do, they spent their time in drinking and gambling.

The sober, hard-working villagers were shocked and angry. The day came when Monsieur Vallé had to speak to Laclede.

"This is very distressing, my friend," he began. "But the people come to me with their complaints. At first they thought it would be a fine thing for you to settle here. Now—well, I will not deceive you. They do not want these men for neighbors."

"No decent people would want them, Vallé," Laclede answered. "I am sick at heart over this business. Of the men with me, there are not more than ten worth having. The others—well, you see what they are. Believe me, they were not my choice. A man with a rich partner cannot please himself, Vallé."

"That's true. Well, no doubt they will sober down after a while. We'll try to make the best of them."

Laclede glanced at his friend. "Perhaps this will not be such bad news to you now. I have

decided that Ste. Geneviève will not do for our settlement."

"Not do? And why not? It has everything you seek."

Pierre Laclede shook his head. "You are proud of your little town, Vallé. I would not hurt your feelings. But I find many objections.

For one thing, Ste. Geneviève lies too low. You tell me yourself that the river floods it every year. For farm land that is not bad. But for a business town, with stocks of merchandise to protect, it is not good."

"But you could build your warehouses farther back, out of the river's reach."

"And out of reach of the docks. No, that would not do. Besides, there is another thing. I want to be nearer the Missouri River. The English control one side of the Mississippi. But the Missouri is in our own territory. I think most of our furs will now come from the Missouri region. The best spot would be near where the two rivers meet. Then we could trade up the Missouri, and ship the skins down the Mississippi to New Orleans."

"Yes, that would be best." Monsieur Vallé looked happier now. He liked Laclede, but he would be glad to see the last of Laclede's followers.

"You will be going on, then?" he asked. "It is getting late in the year. You cannot go much farther before winter."

"I know. That has been troubling me. I

think the best thing would be to go across the river to Fort Chartres. My stores will be safe there under a military guard. We'll stay at the fort until spring. It's not what I wanted, but I don't see anything else to do."

Several men were missing when the time came to start across the river. So were two or three canoes. Laclede, questioning the other men, could learn little. Some had gone down river. Others had simply disappeared into the woods, taking stolen beads and knives with them. Their idea was to set up as Indian traders on their own account. Laclede had only about thirty-five men when he crossed the river.

Fort Chartres was a strong fortress surrounded by a stout stone wall. The French had built it forty years before to protect settlers from the Indians. On either side of the fort were the villages of Cahokia and Kaskaskia. Nearly two hundred French families were divided between the two towns. The fort had a garrison of six or seven hundred men.

Laclede found the commander, Colonel de Neyon, a very troubled man. His fort was now on English soil. His orders were to turn it over to the English army. The trouble was that no English army had appeared. He had no way of knowing when it would come. Until it did, he could not leave his post. Many of the Indian tribes had fought on the English side. They would be sure to make trouble for the French settlers now if De Neyon left them unprotected.

He told his troubles to Laclede over the first evening meal. Laclede himself, with the two boys, was lodged in the commander's cabin. The men had found places in the roomy barracks.

"No, we had no fighting here," De Neyon said, in answer to Laclede's question. "I have spent the war stuck in this dreary hole, while other men gained glory on the battlefield. And now I must surrender without firing a shot! I have had no luck in these accursed colonies. Once I am free of this place, I shall go back to France. I am sick of mud and trees and savages. My eyes ache for the sight of city walls and city streets."

"But we're going to have all that here,"

Auguste interrupted. "That's what we've come for, isn't it, Papa Pierre? To build a city."

"A city? Here? In this savage wilderness?" The colonel snorted. "Laclede, this boy of yours must be simple-minded. A pity. He looks a bright lad too. If he were mine, I'd beat him for such wild talk."

Auguste sighed. It might have been Monsieur Maxent speaking. Now that he thought of it, the fat, fussy colonel even looked like Monsieur Maxent!

What was wrong with these old gentlemen, anyway? Did they think that cities just *grew,* like apples on a tree? Couldn't they see that someone had to start them, sometime? Even Paris, the greatest city of them all. There must have been a time when someone built the first house in Paris. If a great city could rise on the banks of the river Seine, why couldn't another one rise on the banks of the Mississippi River? Why not? Why not?

Auguste was so deep in his angry thoughts that he did not hear Laclede's reply. Soon the talk turned to other matters. Auguste was

glad when the meal was over, and he and
Charlie could slip off to bed.

"I don't like Colonel de Neyon much," he
told his friend as they settled down on their
blankets. The colonel had given Laclede his
guest chamber. The two boys slept on the floor
of an empty storeroom. It was snug and warm,
with the November wind howling outside.

"Neither do I," Charlie answered. "I like
Sergeant Dufour much better. He's the soldier
who helped me get Monsieur Pierre's room
ready. Sergeant Dufour is a fine man. He
fought with General Montcalm. His home is
in Montreal. But when the war was over he
asked to be sent here. He had a special reason
for that."

"You must have had quite a talk! What was
his special reason?"

"Oh, it was a message from a comrade who
died in his arms. The comrade lived near here.
He asked Sergeant Dufour to find his wife and
give her the message. Then when he came
here he found that the wife was dead too. It's
a very sad story."

"Very sad," Auguste agreed. "Charlie, do

you suppose we'll have to stay here all winter?
We couldn't do it if the English came, but
Papa Pierre says they won't come until spring.
He thinks they won't want to bother with a
useless little place like Fort Chartres, with
winter coming on. So we can stay if we want
to. But I don't want to! Shut up inside these
walls, with nothing to do. It's so *dull!*"

"It's warm, though," the Indian boy said drowsily. "Listen to that wind! I'm glad not to be sleeping on the riverbank tonight. And don't worry about having nothing to do, Auguste. I've never known your father to do nothing for very long. Monsieur Pierre will find work for us. Good night."

CHAPTER 6

On the Trail

THE Mississippi Valley winter is mild, but to the visitors from New Orleans it seemed very cold. Early in December Auguste saw his first snow. Sergeant Dufour made a rough sled for the boys. Auguste and Charlie enjoyed coasting on the small hill behind the fort. To them the winter was fun. But Laclede's men cursed the cold and grumbled more than ever.

The first snow melted quickly. After that came several days of bright sunny weather. Colonel de Neyon said this was what the Indians called "squaw summer." It usually lasted all through December. The real winter cold would not set in until after the beginning of the new year.

Laclede asked the colonel many questions about the weather. He also talked to the settlers in the near-by towns. Yes, they all agreed, it was like this every year. The first snowfall. And then a few weeks of clear, mild weather. But after New Year's Day—ah, then the winter began!

"But even then," one old man said, "this year's winter will not be a bad one. I know the signs, Monsieur Laclede. The forest animals have not put on their thickest fur this year. The squirrels have stored only small hoards of nuts. We shall have a soft winter and an early spring."

Laclede listened thoughtfully. The old man had lived in the valley for many years. If the signs told him the winter would be mild, it might be true. Laclede hoped it was true. Perhaps after all he need not waste these winter months.

The leader thought it over and made up his mind. One night at dinner he announced his plan. He was going back to Ste. Geneviève, taking only a couple of men with him. With so small a party he could cover the ground quickly. He would explore from Ste. Geneviève northward toward the Missouri River. Somewhere in that region he would find the site for his city. He would not wait until spring for that.

"A good idea," Colonel de Neyon said. "You can travel with speed, since there will be so few of you. No doubt you will take your two best men. Which ones will they be?"

"Yes, they must be my best men," Laclede said slowly. "They must know how to use an ax and a gun. They must know how to paddle a canoe. All these things are important. But more important still is this: they must be men I can trust. I must know they will do as they are told. I must know they will not desert. They must be men whose whole hearts are in the expedition."

The colonel smiled doubtfully. "And have you such men, Monsieur Laclede? I have seen your followers. I do not think many of them live up to that description."

"There are not many," Laclede agreed. "I

hope there are some. But I am certain of only two. Those two will go with me."

"And which ones are they?"

Laclede looked around the table.

"They are eating your good soup at this minute, Colonel de Neyon."

Auguste and Charlie dropped their soup spoons.

"Papa Pierre!" Auguste gasped. "Do you mean *us?*"

Laclede nodded. "Oh, I know what you would say, Colonel. They are children. But that is not so. My son had his fourteenth birthday in September. Charles is past sixteen. They are young, yes. But they are young men. Look at them! Strong, healthy. Used to hard work and not afraid of it. They proved that on the river. They obey my orders. They do not drink or steal. They do not grumble at hardships."

"But surely these young persons are not skilled woodsmen?" Colonel de Neyon objected.

"No, they are not. But neither are any of the town loafers who came with me. The few good men are townsmen too. A carpenter, a miller, a blacksmith and such. They would be far less useful in the woods than these boys. What Auguste and Charles do not know, I can teach them. They are bright and eager. They will come willingly. That's true, isn't it, boys?"

"Of course it is, Papa Pierre!" Auguste exclaimed. "And there's the other thing you said. About men whose whole hearts are in the expedition. Oh, that's where our hearts are, Papa! We'll show you, won't we, Charlie?"

The Indian boy nodded, unable to speak. That this should come to *him!* He had been kicked around, fed on scraps, treated as Monsieur Maxent's slave. And now Pierre Laclede, with thirty-five men to choose from, had chosen *him!* The others were grown men. White men. But Laclede had chosen Charlie Half-and-Half over all of them!

"When do we start?" Auguste was demanding.

"Tomorrow," Laclede answered. "We'll hope it's true that the winter cold will not set in before the new year. We can finish our mission and return before then."

"We can't do much building in a few weeks, Papa," Auguste objected.

Laclede smiled. "We'll do no building on this trip, son. But we'll find the place to build. Then I can come back here and draw up my plans. As soon as spring comes we shall take the men and their tools to the spot. Then the work can really begin."

Early next morning the three of them

pushed off in Laclede's canoe. Half a day of easy floating and paddling brought them to Ste. Geneviève on the Missouri side. Again they were the guests of Monsieur Vallé.

They stayed overnight in Ste. Geneviève, planning their trip. The Missouri met the Mississippi about seventy miles to the north. They could have gone there by canoe up the Mississippi. But the current was strong at this point, making paddling slow and difficult. Besides that, Laclede was anxious to see something of the land behind the river. He had no way of knowing whether it was forest or prairie. He hoped to find open country, where farms could be laid out. In the end he decided to make the trip on foot.

The first day was easy traveling through the woods, along a trail that led to an Indian village. The Missouris, a branch of the Osage tribe, were friendly to the French settlers. Indians from this village often came to trade at Ste. Geneviève. It was a small place. Half a dozen rush huts clustered on the bank of a little creek. The chief was surprised to see them.

"You come to trade?" he asked in broken French. "It is too early. Our hunts have just begun. We have no skins for you yet."

"We will trade, but not for skins," Laclede answered. He pulled a handful of fishhooks from his pocket. "All we ask is a lodge for the night. Tomorrow we will go."

"You go? Where do you go?"

Laclede waved his hand toward the north. "There. To the banks of the Missouri."

The chief frowned. "To the country of the Sac and Fox? You think they have better furs than ours? It is not so."

Auguste listened carefully as Laclede talked to the chief. Some white men, he knew, treated the Indians with contempt. His stepfather was as polite as if he were talking to a French gentleman.

"Your people bring in fine skins," Laclede was saying now. "I could not find better ones anywhere. But it is as I told you. We are not seeking furs. We want—we want—" He stopped. It was hard to explain. "We want to see what the north country is like," he finished.

To his relief the chief nodded. "Oh, you go to explore. See, I know that word. It is a white man's word. The white man is very curious. He must go. He must see. It is a crazy way to be, we Indians think. But it is the white man's way."

Laclede laughed. "Yes, it's our way. And now will you find us a place to sleep? We must be off early in the morning."

They slept comfortably in the little hut, made of poles covered with mats of woven rushes. Before they set out, Laclede asked the chief for a guide. The Indian shook his head.

"My men would not go into the Sac and Fox country. They are our enemies. We are at peace now. They stay on their lands and we stay on ours. If my man went there, war would come again."

This made sense, as Laclede knew. He had heard of the fierce wars between the Indian tribes. He was glad to know that there was peace now. He would do nothing to start the fighting anew.

"Does it matter, not having a guide?" Auguste asked as they set out.

"I think not," Laclede answered. "He might have found us easier paths. But we cannot get lost. We shall keep the Mississippi on our right, and not stray too far from it. We have only to keep going north until we reach the Missouri. No, we shall do very well without a guide."

And so it proved. They soon found that the trees grew only along the streams. When they left the creeks, they were in open prairie country. The ground was covered with thick grass and weeds, brown and dry in the winter cold. Here and there they came across traces of buffalo herds.

"The buffalo find this good pasture," Laclede said. "That is good. It means our farmers will have wild hay for their cattle. And where these wild plants grow so well, grain will grow too. This is fine farming land. Now we must see how far it extends."

Day after day they pushed forward. Carrying only their light packs and their guns, they made good time. They had brought blankets and a canvas sail for shelter, but no food except frying oil and salt. Their food was all about them—wild prairie chickens, rabbits, squirrels, and fish in the creeks. Laclede was a better shot than the two boys, but they improved under his teaching.

Both boys seemed to take naturally to life in the out of doors. They tramped cheerfully all day, singing their gay songs, making their little jokes. They cooked the meals and ate with good appetite. Auguste was delighted to see how Charlie's skinny frame filled out, now that he had enough to eat. Here on the trail, the Indian boy was remembering little things from his forgotten childhood. The Indian way of fishing, of skinning and preparing game— these seemed to come back to him now. There had always been sadness behind Charlie's good humor. For the first time, it seemed to Auguste, his friend was completely happy.

Pierre Laclede watched the two boys with pleasure. The leader had made many trips before. Never had he traveled with such willing, cheerful companions.

"I made a good choice," he said at the camp-fire one night. "Now that I am sure of that, I may tell you something. At first I was not so sure. I chose you, Charlie, because you are part Indian. I hoped your Indian blood would make this life easy for you. As it has. But Auguste—well, my son, you were used to a comfortable home and your mother's care. I did not know how you would stand this rough living."

Auguste looked at him a minute. Then he laughed.

"Do you think we didn't know, Papa Pierre? You couldn't be sure of anyone, on a trip like this. Certainly you couldn't be sure of *us!* We knew we had to prove ourselves. Well, what do you think of us now?"

"I think very well of you indeed," Laclede answered gravely. "No two men could have done better. I do not know any men who could have done so well. I don't see how I could have done without you."

"Be sure to tell Monsieur Maxent that when we get home," Auguste said with a smile. "Papa," he went on earnestly, "we've been worrying. Will Monsieur Maxent make Charlie come back and work for him?"

The Indian boy looked up.

"I will never go," he said quietly.

"But we have to go back sometime, Charlie," Auguste said. "After all, New Orleans is our home!"

"It is your home, Auguste. It was never mine." Charlie looked around him. They were camped for the night beside a little stream. Big trees crowded around them. Above the trees bright stars looked down.

"I did not know before," Charlie went on. "I was not happy in the city. I thought I was unhappy because I was a poor orphan. That is not true. I am still a poor orphan. But I am happy now. I have been happy ever since we took the trail from Ste. Geneviève. Now I am living as I was meant to live. The woods, the plains, the stars above me—you speak of home, Auguste. This is my home! And I am happy because I have come home."

No one spoke for a few minutes. The fire blazed and died into embers. Laclede looked up.

"Well, time for bed, boys. I want to make an early start."

Two weeks' steady travel brought them to

the banks of the Missouri. They turned east, and then followed the river downstream to the point where it emptied into the Mississippi. In his mind, Laclede had chosen this spot for his city. But when he saw it he shook his head.

"This will not do at all," he said. "There is too much underbrush here for our farms. And the land at the water's edge is marshy. It would be hard to build docks there. No, we must look for another place."

"We could cross the Missouri and go on up the Mississippi," Auguste suggested.

Laclede shook his head. "That is the Sac and Fox country. I hope we shall make friends with that tribe. But it is safer to build in the country of the Missouri Indians. They are already friendly to us.

"No, I think we shall turn southward. We know there is good farming country that way. This time we shall follow the Mississippi River bank. Somewhere on it we will find our site."

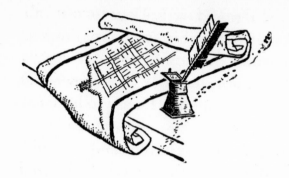

CHAPTER 7

"This Is the Place!"

THEY turned south, back toward Ste. Geneviève. This time they kept close to the Mississippi's west bank. It was hard traveling, for the land was overgrown with thick bushes. There were many stones underfoot. The stones made walking harder, but Laclede was delighted to see them.

"If we build our city near here, we shall have stones for our chimneys," he said.

"Why don't we build it right here?" Auguste asked. "The settlers could cut down the bushes."

"And where would we get logs for our cabins? For that we need big trees. No, this will not do. We must push on."

The bushes were so thick that they could not see what lay ahead. They plodded on, stumbling over the stones, pushing aside the branches that tore their clothing and scratched their faces. In this way they traveled ten miles down the Mississippi. Then on the second day after turning south they found what they were looking for.

It was early afternoon when they pushed their way through the last thicket of bushes. Before them lay a beautiful grove of huge walnut trees. The Mississippi bank rose in a sloping bluff, high enough to be safe from floods. Under the trees, the ground was covered with smooth, short grass. A swift little river, clear as crystal, rushed through the grove, to hurl itself over the bluff and into the Mississippi.

Auguste looked at his father. Both of them spoke at once.

"This is the place!" they cried joyfully.

There could be no doubt of it. This spot had everything they had hoped for. It was on the great river, but high above it. There were trees to give them wood, stones for their fire-places. There was a stream to turn a mill wheel. Inland from the river, as they knew, lay open farming country. Nothing was lacking. They had found the perfect place at last.

Laclede and Auguste threw down their packs. Eagerly they explored the grove. They were too busy to notice that Charlie was not with them.

After a while Auguste left his stepfather among the trees. He was thirsty and went to get a drink from the river. He found the In-dian boy there, kneeling at the water's edge. Charlie scooped the sparkling water in his hand and drank. Then he looked up at Auguste. "The River of the Fathers," he said dreamily.

His friend stared at him. "What do you mean by that?"

Charlie shook his head. His eyes had a far-away look.

"I don't know. The words came to me. I think—I know—I have been here before."

Laclede came up behind the two boys.

"Come, come, no loitering," he said briskly. "There is much to do. We'll make our camp here on the stream. As soon as we have eaten, we'll begin on our plans. Auguste, you have pen and paper in your pack? That's good. I shall need your help."

They ate a hurried meal of cold meat, washed down by water from the stream. As soon as they had finished, Laclede seated Auguste on a flat rock, pen and paper in hand, and he sat near by.

"You draw very well, my boy. Now let me see your best work. Begin by drawing a large map of the grove, just as we see it now. Put in the bluff, the river, and the biggest trees. Show where the grove ends in a belt of thicker forest. Just beyond the forest lie the open lands. Mark these on your map. We won't need to explore them now. We know what they are like, from our journey north. Now, do you understand what I want? Not a pretty picture, as your drawing teacher taught you. But a plain, simple map that we can use as a working plan."

"I understand, Papa. I'll do my best."

While Auguste bent over his map, Laclede and Charlie scrambled down the bluff. First of all they must find a location for their dock.

At the foot of the bluff was a narrow stretch of dry sand.

"Excellent!" Laclede said. "We'll drive

posts out into the shallow water and cover them over to make a log platform. Then a road must be dug out, leading to the higher ground. On this side? No, on this. The slope is gentler here. Um—yes, that's it."

They went back to Auguste, who already had made his rough sketch. Laclede took it and marked the dock site and the curving road. The short road ended at the top of the bluff. Laclede marked a cross at the spot.

"Here we shall build our warehouse," he announced. "Near it there must be houses for our men. Now, let me see. Where shall we put the houses?"

Auguste looked over his shoulder.

"Not too near, Papa. The first street, where the warehouse is, should be a business street. In time there will be many shops there. The homes must be on another street, set back from the river."

Laclede laughed. "Streets, shops, homes— in this wilderness! How they would laugh at us in New Orleans, boy! But you are right. This will be no cluttered frontier village. We are building a city here. It must be properly planned from the first. Very well. This street for shops."

"*Two* streets for shops, Papa," Auguste insisted. "Another street crossing the first one, so that the stores will be close together. Would one more business street be enough, I wonder?"

"I think it will be enough for now," Laclede said with a smile. "There is plenty of room here. Our city can spread out as it grows."

"That's true. But we must be sure to make our streets good and wide. Already the New Orleans streets are too narrow for so many wagons. One day our city will be bigger than New Orleans. We must leave room for all our people."

Laclede nodded, his head bent over the map.

"A fort, and a public square where the soldiers can drill. Here, and here. Also a church. You may choose the spot for the church, Auguste."

The boy put his finger on the map. "I choose this one. And just beside it should be the school."

"A school, of course. I had forgotten that!
You think of everything, Auguste."

"A real city must have a school," Auguste
said seriously.

All through the afternoon they worked
over the plans. They were too busy to notice
that Charlie took little part in their discus-
sions. He sat quietly beside the stream, his
back turned toward them, his eyes on the
rushing water.

The sun was low when Laclede drew the last line on the map.

"Well, there it is. Three long streets, with two others crossing them. All as neat and straight as a checkerboard. A warehouse, a church and school, a public square and a fort. Shops and homes. And outside the woods, acres and acres of fine grassy farm land. What have we forgotten?"

"Nothing but the wall," Auguste answered. "We can use some of the stones we saw. There must be a wall around the settlement, Papa Pierre. All real cities have walls."

"Then a wall there shall be." Laclede took the pen and drew a heavy line, inclosing the checkerboard. He rose and stretched. "Time for supper, boys. Charlie!"

As the Indian boy came toward them, Auguste remembered his strange words some hours before.

"Charlie calls the little river by a name, Papa. What was it, Charlie?"

"River des Pères—River of the Fathers," the boy answered slowly. "I do not know how I know. But that is its name."

"River des Pères?" Laclede repeated. "Why do you call it that?"

Charlie shook his head, and Auguste tried to explain.

"When he saw the little river, he said, 'I have been here before.' That could be so, Papa Pierre. Charlie was found in a ruined village far up the Mississippi. Couldn't that village have been here—right here where we are? I think this is Charlie's old home."

Pierre Laclede had never heard Charlie's story. The two boys told it to him now. How some of Monsieur Maxent's traders had seen smoke arising on the riverbank. How they had come ashore and found the Indian child whimpering in the bushes. How they had taken him with them and given him into the care of Monsieur Maxent's cook.

"And you were how old?" Laclede asked now. "Five, six? I see. But surely you remember something about your life up to then?"

"I remember a great deal, sir," Charlie answered. "The village, the hunt, and how we children fished in a stream. I can see my mother cooking the fish. She told me that my father was a Frenchman, a brave soldier gone to fight for the king. So much I remember. And that dreadful night, when the enemy tribe came—oh, that I can never forget! But I was very young, Monsieur Pierre. I can remember only bits."

"And do you remember this place?" Laclede asked.

"I cannot be sure, Monsieur Pierre. It is the same, and yet not the same. There is no village here. But the river—yes, I am sure of that. The river has not changed. This is where we lived, beside the River des Pères. And this is where my people died."

He spoke so sadly that Laclede laid his hand gently on the boy's shoulder.

"It is all over now, Charlie. They are at peace. You must not grieve for them. And now we must have our supper and get to bed. There will be work for us tomorrow."

They were up early the next morning. There was little more to do here. They would go back and pick up their canoe at Ste. Geneviève. Then cross the river again to Fort Chartres, to wait for spring weather.

Laclede decided not to make the trip back to Ste. Geneviève by land. It would be far easier to float down the Mississippi on a log raft. The strong current would carry them without any effort on their part.

They chopped down half a dozen young trees and trimmed off the branches. The trunks were firmly lashed together. Smaller trees were trimmed down to poles to use in steering. The boys worked well under Laclede's direction. While they worked they talked.

"You'd think we could find some trace of the village," Auguste said. "I've looked hard, but there isn't a sign to be seen."

"I too have looked," Charlie answered. "I found a few blackened stones that may have come from the campfire. But our village was like the one we saw near Ste. Geneviève. It was nothing but a few rush huts. The huts would have burned completely. The enemy would have taken anything useful, weapons and cooking pots. And there would be no— no—" he shivered, and then went on bravely, "there would be no bodies. The enemy always carried them off for their victory cele-

brations. It is their custom. No, it is not
strange that nothing remains here, after ten
long years.''

"Don't think of it any more, Charlie. It was
a dreadful thing, I know. But it's all past and

gone. As Papa Pierre says, your people are at peace now. They were Christians, weren't they?"

"Oh, yes," Charlie answered. "We had no church here. But now and then a priest would come to us. He came in a canoe, perhaps from one of the towns across the river. I don't know. There were always weddings when he came. And the mothers brought their babies to be baptized. I remember hearing Mass under the trees. It must have been these same trees!" Charlie looked up at the leafy roof over their heads. "Yes, they were good Christians, my people. It was a long time between the priest's visits. But we never forgot to say our prayers."

"I suppose a grove does as well as a church," Auguste said thoughtfully. "But we'll have a church here one day, Charlie. And a fort, and a stout stone wall to protect our people. No Indians will ever burn *our* town!"

The raft carried them safely down to Ste. Geneviève. They spent the night with Monsieur Vallé. Again the Ste. Geneviève priest came to dinner. Father Paul had gone to his church at Kaskaskia. Monsieur Vallé said there was great trouble across the river.

"Have the English soldiers come?" Laclede asked.

"Not yet. But every day more English settlers pour in. They are claiming all the best land: farms our French people have worked for years. Their government favors them. Oh, there is no doubt about it. We French will have to get out of English territory. Already most of our people are getting ready to leave."

"And what does Colonel de Neyon say to all this?"

Monsieur Vallé lowered his voice.

"Colonel de Neyon is a very vain man. He won no glory from the war. It is whispered that he has a plan to gain a little glory now. But there, I must not repeat gossip. It is none of my business. But something is being planned across the river, Laclede. Something I cannot approve."

"Well, whatever it is, it won't bother us," Laclede said cheerfully. "We have other things to think about. You will soon have neighbors on this side of the river, Vallé."

"Indeed. That is good news. You have found the site for your city, then?"

"We have found it." Laclede's voice grew solemn. "And on that spot I intend to establish a settlement that hereafter will become one of the finest cities in America."

CHAPTER 8

Trouble Across the River

LACLEDE and the boys reached Fort Chartres in time for dinner that night. Colonel de Neyon came to the table with a frown on his face.

"Things have gone badly while you were away, Laclede," he growled. "Our French settlers don't know which way to turn. It is a good thing they have me to look after them."

"Are the English making trouble?" Laclede asked.

"They are impossible! Impudent, quarrelsome fellows with no respect for authority. Also they are dangerous. They stir up the Indians against us."

He talked on and on, full of hate for the English. Auguste listened with surprise. He had heard his stepfather and Monsieur Vallé discuss the peace treaty. The treaty said that France and England agreed to live in peace. But Colonel de Neyon talked as if the war were still going on. He spoke of England as "the enemy."

The colonel was so full of his own affairs that he scarcely listened to Laclede. What good was a trading post now? he asked. These vile English would ruin trade. Oh, Laclede would see! They would not rest until they had driven the French out of North America. For his part, the colonel said, the English were welcome to it. It was no fit land for white men anyway. It would be better if all Frenchmen returned to France. There a man could live in a civilized way.

Auguste thought the colonel's talk was very tiresome. Laclede must have thought so too, for he left the table early. He said that he had letters to answer.

While they were away, a boat had come up the river from New Orleans. It had brought mail for Pierre Laclede, and one letter for Auguste. Mamma wrote without scolding him. She told him all the news of home. "Be a good boy. Do what Papa tells you. And don't forget your prayers," the letter ended.

It seemed to Auguste he could hear Mamma's loving voice, speaking those words. For a minute he felt very homesick. It had been four months since he left home. That was a long time for a boy to be away. Did he wish he could be home right now? He asked himself the question. There was only one answer. He would love to see Mamma and the little ones again. But not for anything in the world would he miss what lay ahead. The building of a city! Homesick or not, he must not miss his part in that.

Early next morning Pierre Laclede said he was going to Kaskaskia.

"Do you boys want to come?" he asked.

"If you need us, Papa. But we haven't seen Sergeant Dufour yet, and . . ."

"Sergeant Dufour? Oh, yes, that's your soldier friend. No, I shan't need you. Stay here and enjoy yourselves."

As soon as breakfast was over, the boys hurried down to the barracks. They found Sergeant Dufour smoking his pipe under an apple tree.

The sergeant was a burly Frenchman of about forty. Most of his life had been spent in the army. The boys loved his tales of battle and adventure. He was the best friend they had at Fort Chartres.

He was glad to see them this morning.

"So you're back, lads," he said in his gruff voice. "Tell me all your news. Did you find the spot for your city?"

"We found the perfect spot," Auguste said eagerly. "It's on the Mississippi, but it has a little river of its own. The River des Pères. There used to be an Indian village there."

"An Indian village on the River des Pères? I've heard of the place," the sergeant said. "My friend's wife died there. I told you the story, Charlie. About my comrade who was killed at Montreal. I came here to find his wife in the village on the Des Pères. But I was too late. The village was destroyed, and all the people in it."

Charlie looked puzzled. "You did not tell me all this before, sir. You said only that you learned your friend's wife was dead. You did not say she had lived in that village. It cannot be the same place. There was no French lady living there."

"My friend's wife was not French. He married an Indian girl, as many of our traders do. They settled down in her village. They were very happy. Then the war came, and all Frenchmen were called to the colors. He died without ever seeing her again."

The sergeant sighed, thinking of his lost comrade. Then suddenly he asked, "Why did you say no French lady lived there, Charlie? How could you know?"

"I know because that village was my home, sir. When all the others were killed, I alone was left alive."

"But this is a very strange thing!" the sergeant exclaimed. "They told me here at the fort that no one lived through that raid. How did it happen that you escaped?"

Charlie told him the story. The sergeant listened closely, watching the boy's face. He sprang to his feet and beckoned.

"Come here, Charlie. Here in the strong sunlight. How strange that I never noticed before! Your eyes—your hair—Tell me, boy. What is your name?"

"They call me Charlie Half-and-Half, sir."

"Bosh! Your name—your own full name! Do you know it?"

"I do know it, sir. But no one has ever asked me before. Not Monsieur Maxent. Not even my good friend Auguste."

"Well, I ask you now." The sergeant's voice shook with excitement. "If you know, tell me!"

"Yes, sir." The Indian boy threw back his shoulders and stood straight and proud. "I am Charles Louis Ronsard, son of Jean Paul Ronsard, sir."

"Jean! My comrade, my friend! Jean's son! I knew there was a child. He spoke of you with his last breath. 'My love and prayers to my dear wife, and to my little son!' Those were his words. I was to seek her out, and give her those words for comfort. She is gone, but you are here. Jean's son!"

There were tears in the sergeant's eyes. He swept Charlie to him in a mighty hug.

When he was a little calmer, he said, "There

was more to your father's message, Charles. He wanted you to know of your inheritance. In Montreal, just before the battle, Jean had a letter from France. It told him that his father had died, leaving him the family farm. It is your farm now. You have only to claim it."

Auguste looked anxiously at his friend.

"You'd have to go to France to do that, Charlie. You wouldn't leave us to build our city without you. What do you want with a farm in France?"

Charlie was looking a little dazed.

"I am not sure what I want," he said frankly. "This has all been such a surprise."

"There's no hurry," the sergeant said. "If you don't want to go, it could be arranged by some lawyer there. First you'd have to prove that you are really Jean's son. That won't be hard. Jean said that you were christened by the priest who came over from Kaskaskia. No doubt the Kaskaskia church will have a record. You can ask Father Paul about it."

"Well, just don't go rushing off to France," Auguste said. "We can't do without you here, Charlie."

The boys spent the morning with the sergeant under the apple tree. Toward noon Auguste saw his stepfather coming down the trail.

"Come here, Papa Pierre!" he called. "We have exciting news."

Laclede listened with interest to the sergeant's story. He was very glad on Charlie's account, but Auguste could see that his thoughts were elsewhere.

"You have something on your mind, Papa Pierre," Auguste said presently. "Is there trouble in Kaskaskia?"

Laclede nodded. "Much trouble. The French and the English settlers quarrel all the time. Soon it will break into open fighting. And this is what worries me. These men of mine are in the thick of it. They have nothing to do here at the fort. They spend their time in the towns, stirring up trouble. And Colonel de Neyon hasn't been able to stop them."

"Has he tried to stop them, sir?" It was the sergeant's quiet voice. Laclede stared at him.

"What do you mean, man?"

The sergeant cleared his throat. "Monsieur Laclede, it is not my place to speak against my superior officer. But Colonel de Neyon is using your men in a scheme of his own, sir. It is a scheme of which you should know."

"Then tell me. It will go no further, I promise you. We can trust the boys."

"I know that. Sir, our French officers are the finest in the world. I have served under enough of them to know that. But this colonel is a disgrace to us. He thinks only of himself.

He wants to go back to France as a hero. He will take any steps to bring that about."

"But what steps can he take? The war is over. What chance is there to become a hero now?"

"Colonel de Neyon will make his own chance, sir. He finds his chance in the quarrels between the French and the English settlers. He uses the riffraff you brought with you to help the quarrels along. Soon they will drag the Indians into it. When things look really serious, the colonel will step in. He will 'protect' the settlers with military might."

"But this is madness!" Laclede drew a long breath. "It could start the war all over again."

"Not that, sir." The sergeant laughed. "He does not mean to do any fighting. No, he will gather the settlers up and take them to New Orleans under military protection. It will make a fine story—how the brave colonel saved all these innocent people from the wicked English and their Indian allies.

"That is the plan, Monsieur Laclede. Every soldier in the fort knows of it. Most of them like it well enough. They too yearn to be heroes. Me, I do not like it. I fought on the Plains of Abraham. I do not need to play the hero in peacetime!"

"I can't believe it," Laclede said slowly.

"It is hard to believe, sir. But do not take my word alone. Talk to Father Paul at Kaskaskia. He is not blind. He must see what is going on. He will tell you."

"I shall talk to him." Laclede was remembering Monsieur Vallé's words at Ste. Geneviève. "Something planned across the river. Something of which I cannot approve." This must be what he had meant.

"Well, it doesn't concern me," Laclede said now, as he had said then. "I have my own affairs to attend to. Soon we'll begin to build our city. That will keep my men busy."

"That is another thing, sir," the sergeant said. "Not all your men will stay to help you build. From what I hear, most of them plan to go to New Orleans with the colonel. Perhaps they wish to be heroes too."

Laclede rose. "You have given me much to think about, sergeant. For that I thank you. Come, boys, we must go."

The next day Laclede went back to Kaskaskia. He had a long and earnest talk with
Father Paul. Yes, it was all too true, the priest
told him. Laclede's men swaggered in the
town, provoking quarrels with the English.
They went out of their way to insult the Indians who had come to trade. In every possible
way they were stirring up bad feelings.

"And what do your settlers say to all this?"
Laclede asked.

The priest sighed. "The hot-blooded ones are only too eager to join in the quarrels. After all, we French have no reason to love the English! It is easier to break the peace with them than to keep it. And the English here do their part toward breaking the peace. Things are bad, Laclede, and getting worse. I think that sooner or later we French would have to leave. But it is a wicked thing for Colonel de Neyon to add fuel to the flame."

"You think the French must leave Illinois, Father? Where will they go? To New Orleans?"

"I think that is the colonel's plan. The larger the group he takes with him, the greater the glory. But my people love this valley. The boldest of them will not be frightened into leaving it. Many have already crossed the river and settled at Ste. Geneviève. Others will do the same."

"And you yourself, Father," Laclede said. "Where will you go? Wait—don't answer yet. Some of your people want to stay on the Mississippi. Then why can't they come to my new settlement? It is French territory; they will be safe there. It is good farming land. We are planning a church. The flock must have its shepherd. What do you say, Father Paul? Will you come? And will you bring your people with you?"

The young priest's eyes sparkled. "I shall have to ask directions from my superiors at Quebec, Monsieur Laclede. I do not think they will object. I have prayed that my poor people would find a way out of this trouble. I think God has sent you in answer to my prayers!"

Laclede was very thoughtful as he walked home from his visit to Father Paul. Now at last he could have the sort of men he needed so badly. He could get rid of the loafers that he had brought with him.

The next day he called his men together. He paid them their wages for the work already done. Then he told them briefly that those who wished to leave his employment could do so. He would not force them to stay with him any longer.

As he had expected, most of the men were delighted to quit. Twenty-five of them took their pay and hurried away to Kaskaskia. Ten men waited quietly after the others had gone. Several of these were carpenters. The two Taillon brothers were millers. René Kiersereau had taught school. Charles Gratiot was a skilled fur worker.

These were the good men that Laclede had chosen himself. Father Paul would find others like them from among the settlers who wished to stay. Laclede's spirits rose. Ever since he had left New Orleans, he had had to put up with slow, sullen, unwilling workers. Now at last he was free of them. His new city would be built by men with willing hearts and willing hands. With such help he could not fail!

CHAPTER 9

A Boy for a Man's Job

WITH Father Paul's help, Laclede engaged twenty men from among the settlers. He chose the fathers or the grown-up sons of families who wanted to stay in the valley. Pioneer life was not new to these people. They knew what the hardships would be and they would know how to meet them.

The ten men who had come with Laclede had wives and children in New Orleans. Laclede wrote to Monsieur Maxent, urging him to find barges to bring the families and their household goods up the river. He hoped to have everything ready for them before another winter came.

To do that, he would have to make an early start. The mild weather held. The old man had been right when he had said this would be a "soft" winter. Laclede had meant to begin building in March. Now he began to think of an earlier date.

There were other reasons for haste. Life in the fort was not pleasant. Every day there came a fresh report of trouble between French and English settlers. Laclede's discharged men had gone to live in Kaskaskia. Many of the brawls there were of their making. But Colonel de Neyon blamed the English for everything. Openly now he declared to the frightened settlers that only he could save them.

In mid-January the colonel ordered the people to begin building flatboats. These were little more than wooden rafts, big enough to hold furniture and farm implements. Soon everything would be ready for what Sergeant Dufour called "the colonel's grand parade."

Sergeant Dufour told the boys that Colonel de Neyon had decided not to wait for the English army.

"He has always hated the thought of making

the surrender," the sergeant said. "Now, with
the excuse of taking the settlers to safety, he
has found a way out. He'll leave a hundred
men here under young Captain Bellerive.
That will be enough to turn the fort over to
the English when they come. The rest of the
garrison will go with the colonel. It will make
a fine impression when his flatboat fleet sweeps
into New Orleans with a soldier guard. Of
course, he'll have a fine story to go with it.
How the English and Indians were just about
to attack. And how he and his brave men res-
cued the settlers and brought them safely to
New Orleans."

"A fine story," Auguste agreed. "But who
will believe it?"

Sergeant Dufour laughed. "Everyone in the
city will believe it. Why not? The settlers and
the soldiers will tell the same story. Maybe they
believe it themselves. Cowards can believe anything if it gives them an excuse to run away.
Oh, the colonel has no worries. They will
make a great fuss over him in New Orleans.
Perhaps when he goes back to France the king
will decorate him. That is what he hopes for."

"Well, we won't miss him up here," Auguste said with disgust. "The sooner he goes, the better. Captain Bellerive is quite different. I like him."

"Captain Bellerive is a real French officer," answered the sergeant. "We're proud to be under him. I'm staying, of course."

"I thought you would. But you won't be here long, sergeant. What happens after the English army comes?"

"We turn over the fort to them and get out. I don't know where we'll go. But I suppose Captain Bellerive will have his orders."

"I suppose so." Auguste turned away, his face thoughtful.

That night he said to his stepfather, "Papa Pierre, we'll have a fort at our town, won't we? Yes, you put it on the plan. Well, this is what I want to know. Where do we get our soldiers?"

"That is very simple," Laclede answered. "Monsieur Maxent will arrange it with the governor at New Orleans. As French citizens, we have a right to military protection against hostile Indians. The governor will order a garrison for our fort."

"Yes, but where do the soldiers come from?" Auguste persisted. "Will they be sent up from New Orleans?"

"Perhaps. Why do you ask?"

"Because — because — well, see here, Papa Pierre. Captain Bellerive and his men will leave Fort Chartres when the English soldiers come. Why can't we have *them* for our fort? They know this country. They like it up here. Sergeant Dufour said they would be given a choice. Those who wish may go to New Orleans with the colonel. The hundred men who stay behind are staying willingly. And they're the fort's best men, Papa!"

Laclede smiled. "I take it your friend the sergeant is one of them? Well, this is a good idea, Auguste. I'll mention it when I write to Monsieur Maxent."

By the first of February, Laclede's plans were complete. There had been a bit of good luck. The old man who ran the mill at Kaskaskia was anxious to get back to New Orleans. He would sell his mill at a reasonable price. Laclede had millers with him, but no mill machinery. He took the Taillon brothers to see the Kaskaskia mill. They found it in good shape. Laclede decided to buy the machinery and set it up on the River des Pères.

Everyone was anxious to get away. There seemed no reason to linger. Early in February Laclede began loading his two barges with tools and supplies. The day of departure was set.

The old men and the new ones worked cheerfully over the loading. Auguste was everywhere, lending a hand, cracking a joke, starting a song to make the work go faster.

The hardest job was loading the great stone mill wheel. A team of oxen dragged it to the dock. Laclede rigged a rope and pulley to swing it aboard. It landed on one side, tipping the barge dangerously. Laclede ordered it pulled up again, and he himself jumped aboard to direct it toward the center.

It was late in the afternoon. The light was failing. In some way that no one ever understood, the pulley slipped. The heavy stone came down with a crash, just missing Laclede's head. As he leaped aside, one foot was caught and pinned under the crushing weight.

The men carried him into the fort, and the
army doctor came. Several bones of the foot
were broken. The foot itself was badly torn
and bruised. The doctor said it would be weeks
before he could stand on it.

Auguste was hovering anxiously by the bed-
side. He could see that his father was in great
pain.

"What can I do to help, Papa Pierre?" he asked. "Only tell me. I'll do anything!"

"Anything?" Pierre Laclede managed a smile. "I'll take your word for that, Auguste. Bring the men to me. Yes, all of them. The Thirty. Get them here quickly."

The thirty men crowded into the chamber. Laclede, his bandaged foot propped up on pillows, spoke briefly.

"We'll waste no words, men. I cannot go with you tomorrow. But there will be no delay. My son will take my place."

Auguste gasped, but Laclede went on: "Auguste knows the plans as well as I know them myself. If I did not trust him I would not send him. I expect you to put yourselves under his orders, to serve him as you would serve me. If any man here objects to Auguste Chouteau as his leader, let him speak now."

There were surprised grins, but no words until the elder Taillon spoke.

"Master Auguste is young, sir, but we do not hold that against him. He suits us very well as a leader." Taillon looked around. The other men nodded. "I speak for all of us, Master

Laclede. We will follow the boy as we would follow you, sir."

One by one the men came forward to shake Laclede's hand and wish him a speedy recovery. Then they filed out, and Laclede was left alone with his son.

"Well, Auguste?"

"I—I don't know what to say, Papa Pierre. You have taken my breath away. But if you think I can do it . . ."

"Certainly you can do it. Say no more about it, boy. It's settled now. Get the plan of our town, Auguste. I must go over it with you once again."

They bent over the map Auguste had drawn, while Laclede made sure that the boy understood all that was to be done. Presently Pierre Laclede put his finger on a spot near the church.

"Do you remember this place, Auguste? As I recall it, there was a hill here and some especially fine walnut trees. A good place for a house. Mamma likes a shady garden. Yes, a good place for our house. Put it there."

"Our house? Oh, Papa Pierre!" Auguste's

eyes shone. "I did not know—I did not dream! We are to *live* in our city? Not just build it for others? It will be our home? You never told me this."

"I have only lately made up my mind, Auguste. Yes, I shall bring Mamma and the children here. Monsieur Maxent can take care of affairs in New Orleans. It is important for me to be here to deal with the Indians; to see that all goes well with the settlers. As soon as we have a shelter for them, I will send for Mamma and the children."

"And I am to build their house. Here, where you have marked the map."

"Yes, build it there, Auguste. It need not be very big. We'll all have to be content with small cabins at first. They can be quickly built. Later, when there is more time, we shall put up permanent homes."

"Yes, Papa." Auguste's face was very serious. "I don't know how well I can do this. It's a big job. But it's the job you've given me. I shall do my best."

The start was made next day. The men towed the barges upriver to a point just opposite the chosen spot. Then, with oars and poles, they moved the laden boats across the river. They brought them safely to the sandy beach below the bluff. It was St. Valentine's Day. On that date, February 14, 1764, a great city was born.

The men tied up the barges and waited for orders. Auguste looked into their faces and smiled.

"I guess you're wondering what it will be like to work under a boy," he said. "Well, I'll tell you. You're not working for me. You're not even working for my father. You're working for yourselves. Your wives and children will live in the houses you will build. You want your children to grow up in a clean, orderly place, with sound roofs over their heads. You want a church and a good school for them. Well, we're going to have those things here. You men are going to put them here."

He paused, and the men nodded their agreement.

"That's enough about that," Auguste went on. "Now there's something else I want to say. We'll work hard here. But we'll have fun doing it. Maybe, being only fourteen, I think more about fun than you men who are older. And maybe 'fun' isn't the right word. 'Adventure' is better. For this is an adventure for me, for all of you. Think what it means, men! My father says the city we shall build here will one day be one of the world's great ones. Who knows the names of the men who built Paris, or London, or even New Orleans? No one. But your names are known. Taillon, Kiersereau, Gratiot, and all the rest—those names will go down in history. When you are dead, yes, centuries after you are in your graves, your names will live! Do you see why I call this a wonderful adventure?"

They listened, and looked at him, and smiled at each other. He was so earnest about all this, Laclede's lad, with his talk of a great city. Who ever heard of a city rising in this savage land? Kaskaskia, Cahokia—they were old towns now, and very little larger than when first settled. Certainly they had not become great cities. Why should this one be different? A good little settlement, yes. The boy spoke sense when he reminded them that they must make it a good one for the sake of their families who were coming. But a great city, never! Such things did not happen.

They hid their amusement, for they liked the boy. Let him keep his dream. Little Master Auguste, with his high-flying notions! These did no harm. And it was plain he would not be a harsh taskmaster. The word he had first used came back to their minds. Adventure this might not be. But working with Auguste would certainly be fun.

It was two months before Laclede was able to leave the fort. His foot was soon healed, but he was delayed by the confusion of the colonel's arrangements. In mid-April the "grand parade" finally moved off down river. Colonel de Neyon took with him more than a hundred families, the settlers he had "saved." They were escorted by five hundred uniformed soldiers, marching along the bank with their bayonets gleaming. Laclede heard later that New Orleans gave the party a welcome that lived up to all the colonel's hopes.

The last barge was scarcely out of sight when Laclede had to receive a visitor. Monsieur Maxent arrived without any warning. He came in a comfortable large boat, rowed by six sturdy oarsmen. The boat was well stocked with cushions and a feather bed, and a fine supply of food. But at dinner that night, the old gentleman could talk of nothing but the hardships of his journey.

"This is a barbarous country," he said angrily. "To think that I, a gentleman of France, was forced to make my bed upon the ground! Never have I endured such misery. And the sun! The mosquitoes! Oh, my friend, you cannot imagine how I suffered."

Laclede hid a smile as he answered. "It is a tiring journey, sir. I wonder that you gave yourself the trouble to come. There was no need."

"No need!" Monsieur Maxent snorted. "There was every need. I had to see for myself what goes on up here, Laclede. I must tell you that your letters have been very upsetting. You yourself, you wrote, had been crippled in an accident. Even the accident I do not understand. A millstone crushed your foot. What have you to do with millstones? You are an Indian trader, not a miller! No, no, do not trouble to explain. The millstone, that is a small matter.

"But there is another matter that is not small. If I read your letter aright, you have sent a child to build our trading post. I could scarcely believe my eyes! A little boy—a baby—

a whimpering infant to command grown men!
So I understood you to write. I can only hope
you will tell me that it is not true."

"I can certainly tell you that, Monsieur
Maxent." Laclede spoke quietly, but his eyes
flashed. "My son Auguste is no infant, and he
does not whimper. If I did not know he could
handle the job, I would not have given it to
him. You will find that he and Charles have
done all that I could have done."

"Charles! That is another thing. You are
harboring a runaway slave, Laclede. I do not
say the boy is a thief, although he took a valu-
able canoe when he left my house. But . . ."

"But he left a silver snuffbox in payment,"
Laclede added. "No, you cannot say he is a
thief, sir. And you know very well that he was
never your slave. A runaway, yes. Perhaps you
will blame me for not sending him back. Very
well. I accept the blame for keeping him and
for keeping my son also. You placed me in
charge of this expedition. I gave these two
boys a chance to prove their worth. They have
proved it over and over."

The old man made an angry gesture, but

Laclede went on, speaking in his pleasant, friendly voice. "Come now, Monsieur Maxent, let us not quarrel. We are partners. All that I have done, I have done for the good of our undertaking. You are tired from your long journey. A good night's sleep tonight, and you will feel better. Tomorrow you shall see the new settlement for yourself. I do not think you will be displeased with it."

"Well, well, we shall see," Maxent grumbled. "As you say, I must have rest. The meal was not bad, not bad at all for this wilderness. Now I hope you have a decent bed for me."

Monsieur Maxent was in a better humor at breakfast time. When his servants had placed the cushions to his satisfaction, he squeezed himself into Laclede's canoe.

Laclede was silent as he paddled up and across the river. He earnestly wished he could have paid his first visit to the settlement without Maxent. In the two months since Auguste had left, a canoe had twice come across the river to carry back food and building supplies. Each time the messenger reported that the

work was going well. Laclede himself felt sure
he would be satisfied with what Auguste had
done. But would Monsieur Maxent be satisfied? And if he were not, what would he do?
Pierre Laclede was a very worried man.

Intent on his paddling, he scarcely looked
up as they approached the west bank. He was
startled by an exclamation from his partner.

"Laclede! This cannot be the place. Look,
we are approaching a town. I see buildings,
and a dock. You must have lost your way on
the river."

"I think not." Laclede smiled, and then
shouted. A man working on the dock looked
up. He dropped his hammer and hurried to
the water's edge. Laclede recognized him as
one of the carpenters.

"Well, Rodin, how goes it?" he asked, as he
stepped out of the canoe.

The man bowed, eying Monsieur Maxent's
purple velvet coat with some curiosity. "It
goes very well, Monsieur Pierre. But we are
not yet in good shape for visitors. Nothing is
really finished except the warehouse and the
dock. I was just setting the last log here. It is

E.F.CORTESE

a good dock, is it not? Strong, see?" He stamped heavily on the stout logs.

"Very good," Laclede agreed. "But we find you alone. Where are my son and the others?"

"Master Auguste and the men are in the woods today cutting timber," Rodin answered. "Come, sirs, and repose yourselves in the warehouse. There are chairs there. And I will go for Master Auguste."

He led the way up the bluff. It was a steep climb under the hot spring sun. When they had reached the high ground, they saw the half-finished town spread out before them. The checkerboard streets of the map were marked out with ropes stretched between stakes. On each lot a log cabin was rising. Some were nearly done, lacking only roof and chimney. A line of stones showed where the walls of the fort would stand.

The warehouse stood just at the top of the bluff. Rodin opened the door and stepped aside for the visitors to enter first.

"Here are chairs, gentlemen. I hope the warehouse pleases you, Monsieur Pierre. We use it as our living quarters now. It seems very large to me, but Master Auguste would have it so. And now, if you will excuse me, I go to fetch him."

Monsieur Maxent sank into the nearest chair. The older man's face was red from the heat, and streaming with perspiration. He was still puffing from the climb up the bluff.

"Well, sir?" Laclede said anxiously. "You can see for yourself. All this has been accomplished in two months' time. What do you think of it?"

"I think nothing as yet," Maxent answered crossly. "My head is swimming from the glare of the sun on the water. It is necessary that I rest myself. One must think of his health."

"Of course, sir." Laclede looked around him. The warehouse walls were lined with wooden bunks. "Here is a bed that looks comfortable, and the blankets seem clean. Why do you not take a little nap? Then, when the sun is lower, we can inspect the settlement. We must not risk a sunstroke for you. As you say, you must take care of your health."

With a grunt Maxent accepted the suggestion, stretching out on the bunk. In a few minutes his snores announced that he was safely asleep. Leaving the dim cool warehouse behind him, Laclede stole out and closed the door. Thank heaven, he could now have his first talk with Auguste alone.

CHAPTER 10

Monsieur Maxent Sees the Light

LACLEDE stood for a moment outside the warehouse door. The only signs of life were afar off. There, toiling up a hill, a line of Indians could be seen. Each was carrying a heavy stone. A man in Frenchman's clothing was directing them.

Puzzled, Laclede walked toward the hill. He had heard nothing of the presence of any Indians at the town site. As he drew nearer, the leader turned and saw him. He came scrambling down the hill. It was Charlie.

"Monsieur Pierre!" he cried. "Oh, this is a pleasant surprise! Does Auguste know you are here?"

149

"Rodin has gone to the woods to tell him," Laclede answered.

"Then he should be here soon. And in the meantime, sir, let me be the first to welcome you to St. Louis."

"St. Louis?" Laclede said. "You have found a name for our town, then?"

"We wanted to give it your name, sir," Charlie said shyly. "But Auguste thought Monsieur Maxent might be jealous. And we certainly didn't want to call it after him. So Auguste chose St. Louis. He says even Monsieur Maxent can't find fault with a saint's name. If you do not approve, we shall leave it to you to find another. But we think it is a good name for a French town. St. Louis was a French saint, wasn't he, Monsieur Pierre?"

"He was indeed," Laclede answered. "A Crusader king of France. And he is the patron saint of our present king, Louis XV. Yes, it is a good choice, Charlie. St. Louis it shall be. But tell me now, what goes on here? What are those Indians doing up there?"

Charlie hesitated. "I think Auguste will

want to tell you about that, sir. Will you wait to hear it from him?"

"Very well." While they talked, they walked slowly between a line of half-finished cabins. Laclede looked around him with approval.

"You have done far better than I expected," he remarked. "Some of these houses are almost ready to move into."

"The men have worked very hard on their homes," Charlie answered. "They are anxious to have their families here. We think we can be ready for the wives and children by midsummer."

"Midsummer, you say? I had not hoped for that. I thought it would be late autumn by the earliest before we could send for the families. Look, isn't that Auguste there among the trees? Yes, it is. Auguste!"

At his father's shout Auguste turned and came running toward them. "Papa Pierre! Oh, it is good to see you! And your foot? Is it well?"

"Quite well, my boy. Catch your breath now, for I want you to tell me all about your city of St. Louis."

"You like the name then, Papa? And you will like the town as well. What have you shown him, Charlie?"

"Nothing at all, except some of the cabins," Charlie answered.

"Good. Then come along, Papa Pierre. You must see everything."

"If you will excuse me, I will get back to my work."

Charlie bowed and left them.

Eagerly Auguste led the way from one point to another. On the bank of the River des Pères, the frame of a flour mill was rising. The great stone wheel was already in place.

"The Taillon brothers are in the woods to-day, cutting logs," Auguste explained. "You can't imagine how splendid the men have been, Papa. Everyone turns his hand to everything. The two millers are our best tree choppers. And Kiersereau, who never held a hammer before, has become a fine carpenter. They work from sunup to sundown, and never a word of complaint. They know they are working for themselves, that's why. They are building a good town for their children to grow up

in. Nothing is too much trouble if it makes the town better.

"Come this way now. Here is to be our church. Have you heard whether Father Paul can come to us?"

"Yes, I have good news for you, Auguste. Father Paul's superiors have assigned him to the church here. There is more good news, too. Sergeant Dufour sent a message. He says to tell you he will see you soon. Captain Bellerive has orders to move his garrison here, as soon as the English arrive."

"Oh, how wonderful! We'll begin on the fort as soon as Charlie's Indians finish what they are doing."

"I think you'd better leave the fort to Captain Bellerive and his men," Laclede said. "After all, we are not military architects. But by the way, what *are* Charlie's Indians doing now? He said you would tell me about this yourself."

"Yes, I want to tell you. But not now. It's a surprise, and I'm keeping it for the last. Now here, beside the church, will be our school. Kiersereau was a teacher in New Orleans, you know. We thought he could teach the children here."

Laclede agreed. He followed Auguste up and down the unfinished streets, carefully inspecting all that had been done. He could find no fault with anything. The men from the Illinois settlements knew how to build log cabins, for they had built them before. They had made these new ones bigger and better than the ones they had left behind. The wives, when they arrived, would have cause to be proud of their new homes.

When Papa Pierre and his son had seen everything else, Auguste led the way toward the little hill.

As they came closer to it, they could see that a wide, shallow hole had been dug out at the top. Charlie was down in the hole, carefully laying stones around the edges. He jumped out and came toward them.

"Have you told Monsieur Pierre yet?" he asked Auguste.

"I am just about to tell him. Look, Papa Pierre. This is our house. It won't be an ordinary log cabin. It will be a real French house, built of stone. Charlie is beginning the cellar now. We found the house plans in a book of Kiersereau's. There will be two stories, with a fine shady gallery all around, so that Mamma can take the air on hot days. Oh, Mamma will be proud of her house, Papa Pierre! It will be as grand as any house in New Orleans. Yes, it

will be grander than Monsieur Maxent's.
What will he say to that?"

"We shall soon know." Laclede smiled, but
his eyes were serious. He glanced toward the
warehouse with its closed door. Auguste had
kept the house as a surprise. Well, he had a
surprise too. It might not be such a pleasant
one as Auguste's. But he would keep it a little
while longer.

"It is a house to be proud of," he said cheerfully. "And now perhaps you will explain
about these people who are working on it.
Where did you find your Indian labor,
Auguste?"

"Charlie's Indian labor," Auguste said with
a laugh. "The Indians won't work for me,
Papa. Only for Charlie. This is how it happened. Only last week these people came
down the Missouri River in canoes. They
were fleeing from an enemy tribe that had
burned their village. When they saw that we
were white men, they asked for our protection. We said they could camp here, and their
enemies have not followed them. When they
knew that they were safe, I tried to offer them

jobs. But they didn't want to work. Then Charlie talked to them, and they agreed. They are doing all the work on your house. Charlie told them it was for a Great White Chief who would bring soldiers to keep their enemies away forever. Of course, we're paying them too, in buttons and calico."

"They are good people," Charlie said. "They trap and hunt, but they know how to farm too. Our settlers can learn much from them. They want to stay here. Not in a white man's town, of course. But they plan to settle beyond the woods if you will allow it, Monsieur Pierre."

"Why not?" Laclede asked. "There is room for all, white men and red. And with our fort here, they will be safe from their enemies."

"I am glad to hear you say that, Monsieur Pierre," Charlie said. "I could not promise the Indians that they could stay until you gave permission. It will make them very happy."

"And it makes Charlie happy too," Auguste said with a laugh. "The Indians are his friends, Papa Pierre. Sometimes I think he likes them better than he does Frenchmen."

"You must not say that, Auguste," Charlie said gravely. "You are my best friend in this world. Monsieur Pierre is my friend, and Sergeant Dufour, and Father Paul. Yes, and all The Thirty are my friends. You are of my father's people. But it is true that I feel drawn also to the people of my mother. Is there any harm in that?"

"Of course there isn't," Auguste said warmly. "Can't you take a joke, Charlie? I think it is fine that you get along so well with the Indians. If you didn't, you'd probably be going off to France to live, instead of . . . Oh, but I forgot. We haven't told Papa Pierre yet what you have decided to do."

Laclede looked puzzled. "Something that Charlie has decided? About what, may I ask?"

"About his farm in France, Papa. Don't you remember? The one his grandfather left him. I was afraid he'd want to go to France and live on the farm. But he has a better plan. He's going to have the lawyer there sell the farm and send him the money. And with the money—go on, Charlie. It's your plan. Tell Papa Pierre about it."

Charlie raised his eyes to Laclede's face. "It is like this, sir. As Auguste says, I want to invest my money here. I thought I would use it to buy a stock of trade goods. Then I could go up the Missouri and buy furs to sell here in St. Louis. The Indians trust me, for I am one of them. They will deal with me more willingly than with a Frenchman. I am not happy in a city, Monsieur Pierre. I love the Indian life, the life of the streams and the forest. Yet half my heart will always be here, with Auguste and the town we have built. It seems to me that in this way I can have the best of both, a white man's life and an Indian's life. I do not know what you will think about this, sir. I ask your advice."

"Why, it seems to me a very good plan," Laclede answered. He thought for a moment. "You will buy a stock of trade goods, you say? And later you will have furs to sell? I wonder— yes, I think . . ." He laughed suddenly. "I had forgotten, Charlie, that you are now a young man of property. This will make a difference, if I know my partner."

He looked into the puzzled faces of the two

boys. "You think I am talking in riddles? Well, never mind. We shall soon learn the answer. Yes, your plan is a good one, Charlie. There is only one difficulty. And if you will leave it to me, I think I can overcome it."

"That's fine." Auguste looked up at the sun. "It's time to begin dinner, Charlie. The men will be coming in from the woods."

Charlie spoke to the Indians, who stopped work and moved off to their camp. Auguste led the way to the warehouse.

"Charlie and I are still the cooks," he explained. "You don't know how glad we'll be to see the men's wives come. But if we expect good work we have to provide good food. And it seems that we are the only ones who know how to cook it."

As Auguste started to open the door, Laclede laid a hand on his arm.

"Softly, my son. Do not make too much noise. Monsieur Maxent is asleep inside."

Auguste jumped back.

"Monsieur Maxent! Papa Pierre, you are joking."

"Not at all. Just a minute before we go in.

I would like you to manage the cooking by yourself tonight, Auguste. It will be better if my partner does not see Charlie at such work just now. Oh, I know this sounds very mysterious, but you will soon understand. Charlie, your face and hands are smeared with mud. Run down to the river and wash yourself. And comb that wild mop of hair. I'd like to see you looking as smart as possible when you return."

"Yes, sir." Charlie turned away, but Laclede called him back.

"One more thing. Do not be surprised at anything you hear me say. Try to act as if you had known it all along. That's all. Run along, now."

Drawing a long breath, Laclede motioned Auguste to open the door.

Monsieur Maxent sat up at the sound of their footsteps. "Where am I?" he muttered.

Laclede came forward with a smile.

"You have had a good sleep, my friend. And now you are ready for your dinner. It will not be long. Auguste, let us move some chairs out into the fresh air. The sun is low, and it is cooler now."

Soon Maxent was comfortably settled under a walnut tree, a bottle of wine beside him. The gentleman from New Orleans was no drunkard. But he was fond of wine, and a glass often helped to calm his hot temper. Laclede wanted to do everything possible to keep him in good humor tonight.

Laclede took the second chair and filled the glasses. Indoors, Auguste began the bustle of getting dinner. Soon the good smell of jugged hare floated out on the evening breeze. Maxent sniffed. His fat face took on a pleasanter expression.

"The nap has refreshed me," he admitted. "And I find myself in good appetite. The young man seems to be a capable cook. Who is he, Laclede? One of the Kaskaskia settlers?"

"No, indeed. That is my son Auguste, the leader of the expedition. You may think it odd that he does the cooking. But like all good leaders, he thinks first of the well-being of his men. Good work deserves good food, he says. He gives his men good food, and they work well."

"That is wise," Maxent nodded. "But Laclede, you amaze me. This is your son? This is the child who ran away to join you? How can that be? Why, he is taller than I am!"

"It is ten months since last you saw Auguste, sir. Yes, he has grown tall in those months. I don't wonder that you did not recognize him. And here, coming toward us, is someone else you may know." He raised his voice. "Charles!"

Maxent's jaw set. "Yes, I know that one at sight. And I have some words to say to him. Here, you! Come here!"

Charlie's head was high as he walked toward them. He had washed his face and smoothed his hair and brushed the dust from his clothes. Laclede, watching him approach with his quick, graceful step, thought he was a fine figure of a young man.

Charlie came close to the two men, and bowed.

"Good evening, Monsieur Maxent. You called me, Monsieur Pierre?"

"*I* called you, boy!" Maxent said violently. "I, your master! I demand an explanation of your conduct. You dared—you dared—" his anger almost choked him. "Wretch, ungrateful creature! Oh, wait until I get you back to New Orleans! You shall see how we deal with such criminals."

Charlie spoke quietly but very firmly.

"You are no longer my master, Monsieur Maxent. Nor am I a criminal. It is true that you gave me shelter when I was a helpless child. For that I owed you a debt. I paid that debt by years of unpaid toil in your service. Now I am a free man. I shall never go back to New Orleans."

"You dare to say that! Of course you will go. Yes, if I have to bring a squad of soldiers from Fort Chartres to make you! Laclede, this is your doing. Well, now you can undo it. Seize this young rascal and bind him at once. We'll take him back to the fort with us."

"Let us not be hasty, sir," Laclede said mildly. "First there is a matter of business to discuss."

"Business? What business? Explain yourself, Laclede."

"Gladly. Since you saw Charles last, his position has changed. He is now a young man of property. A very considerable property, I may say. He has inherited a very large farm in France. Charles does not intend to work the farm. He proposes instead to sell it and invest his money here on the Mississippi."

"Indeed?" Maxent leaned forward in sudden interest. "And may one ask what is the value of this farm?"

"That we do not know. Charles has yet to

claim his property and arrange for the sale. But undoubtedly it will bring him a tidy sum. With this money he thinks of going into Indian trade. However, as you know, he cannot become a trader here without your permission. The king has given you the sole right to buy furs from the Indians. You can grant that right to Charles. With his own money he can buy trade goods from you, and sell you the furs he obtains. It would be a good business arrangement for all of us. What do you think of it?"

Maxent was silent, and Charlie's heart sank. He had made his plan without remembering that Maxent controlled the right to trade. If he refused his permission, the plan could not be carried out. This was the one difficulty of which Laclede had spoken. Charlie glanced at Laclede and met an encouraging smile.

It seemed ages until Monsieur Maxent spoke. When he did, Charlie could scarcely recognize the hearty, friendly voice.

"Well, my boy, this is a very fine thing. Let me congratulate you on your good fortune. Yes, as Laclede says, this will be a good business arrangement for all of us." Then, as Charlie did not answer, he grew a little anxious. "Perhaps I spoke hastily just now," he went on awkwardly. "If so, I meant no offense. Now that we are to do business together, we must be friends. Is it not so?"

Before Charlie could answer, Laclede spoke quickly.

"Of course, Charles need not go into the fur business. The Indians have other things to sell. To the north, around Detroit, there are iron mines. It may be that Charles would prefer to buy iron and sell it in Detroit. In that case, he would find it more convenient to deal with some Detroit firm."

Charlie gasped in astonishment, and Laclede frowned him to silence. Monsieur Maxent noticed neither of them.

"Oh, no," he was saying in a voice that shook with alarm. "No, no, that would never do. Those rascals in Detroit would soon rob the dear lad of all his fortune! Tell him, Laclede, he must not be so foolish. How much better it will be for him to deal with us, his old friends whom he can trust! Charles, my dear young friend, surely you must see that your best interests lie with us.''

Charlie could scarcely believe his own ears. Monsieur Maxent was pleading with him—with Charlie Half-and-Half! Only a year ago he had been afraid of this fat, greedy little man. Now he could almost feel sorry for him. Monsieur Maxent had no wife, no children, no one who cared two pins for him. All he had was his business. All he could think of was making money. How could one go on hating such a lonely, unloved person?

The Indian boy put out his hand. "Monsieur Maxent," he said gently, "you have often been harsh with me. Perhaps I was not always a good servant. Those days are past and we will not speak of them again.''

"Then it's a bargain!" Maxent sprang up and grasped Charlie's hand. "We'll have a talk later, my boy. I have friends in France. I can hurry the matter of getting your money to you. You propose to go among the Indians yourself? Yes, yes, that is good. Your Indian blood will be a great help there. Laclede, I think we've done a fine stroke of business today.''

"I think so too." Laclede stood up and stretched his long legs. He had not been at all sure how this conversation would turn out. Now it was happily ended, to the satisfaction of everyone. He put an affectionate hand on Charlie's shoulder.

"Auguste is setting the tables under the trees. It must mean that dinner is nearly ready. No doubt he can use your help now."

But even as he spoke, Auguste turned and called to them. The two seats of honor, at the head of the larger table, were reserved for Laclede and Maxent. The boys disappeared into the warehouse, and Laclede could hear wild bursts of laughter as Charlie related his interview with Maxent. Then, with sober faces, the boys came out, carrying great bowls of soup.

From the woods came the tramp of many feet. Soon The Thirty came into view. They were tired and hungry, but in high spirits. Lusty voices were raised in song:

"Tonight we eat roast duck, fal la,
Tonight we eat roast duck!"

CHAPTER 11

St. Louis, U. S. A.

LACLEDE and Monsieur Maxent stayed with Auguste a few days longer. No one could have believed that the visit would go so well. Maxent had never been able to understand why Laclede wanted to build a town instead of just a trading post. Now, as he walked the streets of a real town, he began to see the reason. As Auguste pointed out, the town would not live by the fur trade alone. When the men would get their farms started, there would be grain to ship to New Orleans. There were herds of elk and buffalo near by, and these hides made good leather. St. Louis could have a tannery, and prepare the leather there.

170

Timber, too, could be cut and floated down the river.

This was the sort of talk that Monsieur Maxent understood. Business to be done. A profit to be made. He listened approvingly to Auguste's plans. Soon he began pointing out to Laclede what a bright young man Auguste was. What a business head he had on his young shoulders!

Such a leader of men too, Monsieur Maxent added. He had talked to the men of The Thirty, and had heard nothing but praise for Master Auguste. Never before, they had told him, had they worked under a leader who made work a pleasure. The day went by in song and joke, with a meal to finish it off that the king might envy. Yes, The Thirty agreed, this would be a fine town, this St. Louis. And it was all Master Auguste's doing.

"I wish the men wouldn't praise me so much to Monsieur Maxent," Auguste told his father. "It makes me uncomfortable. And it isn't true, Papa Pierre. *You* found the place; *you* drew up the plans for the town. I did nothing but carry out your orders. But the men are making Monsieur Maxent believe that I did everything."

Laclede laughed. "As long as your own head is not turned, my boy, I do not mind. The important thing is that we have won Monsieur Maxent over. He is as impatient as you are to see the town grow. He spoke to me this morning about the families of the men who came from New Orleans. As soon as he goes back, he will find barges to bring them here. The other families, those across the river, can come whenever you are ready for them."

"We'll be ready in July," Auguste said happily. "Papa Pierre, the boats from New Orleans will bring Mamma and the little ones, won't they? Oh, it will be good to see them again! Do you think Mamma will like her house? Does she want to live in St. Louis?"

"She wants to live where we are, Auguste. Yes, St. Louis will be our home, and our children's home, and the home of their children for all the years to come. It is not a small thing that we have done here, my boy. The world may laugh at us now. But one day the world will know that ours was no idle dream. One

day the world will see that you and I have built a great city."

The next day Laclede took Maxent back to Fort Chartres and saw him on his way down the river. Laclede spent the next few months helping to finish the building of the town. Early in July, as Auguste had promised, everything was ready for the families.

They arrived on a glorious summer day. Monsieur Maxent came from New Orleans with Madame Laclede and the children. Their barge touched at Fort Chartres to pick up Father Paul. As they approached St. Louis, Maxent began to point out the sights.

"Your church, Father Paul—you can see the steeple from here. And there, Madame, set on the hill, the stone house is yours. A very fine house it is, let me tell you. Built entirely by Indian labor. Not everyone can induce the savages to work. But Monsieur Charles Ronsard is a wonder with them. Do you know Monsieur Ronsard, Father? An excellent young man. He was once in my employ. Now he is going into business for himself. Ah, youth, youth! What fine young people we have nowadays! There is your son Auguste, Madame Laclede, a lad in a thousand! He will go far, that boy. I predict a great future for him."

"I am glad to hear you say so, Monsieur." Auguste's mother spoke absently, her eyes on the shore. There, waving joyfully, was her husband. But the young man beside him, so tall, so handsome—could that really be her little Auguste? He caught sight of her, and smiled. Yes, it was, it really was!

The mother turned her beaming face to Father Paul.

"The boy looks well, Father."

The good priest laughed. "Don't try to hide your pride, my daughter. You have a right to feel proud. Yes, that is your son. And there behind him lies his city. May our Heavenly Father bless this fair city of St. Louis. And may His blessing fall upon its first citizen, Auguste Chouteau."

Afterword

Just forty years later, in 1804, the Louisiana Purchase made Missouri a part of the American Republic. The United States Government sent an army captain named Stoddard to explain the change to the people of St. Louis.

Captain Stoddard found a happy, prosperous town surrounded by fertile farms, the center of the valley's fur trade. It was not a city yet, but it was on its way.

Laclede was dead now, and Monsieur Maxent, and most of The First Thirty. Charles Ronsard, although he came often to St. Louis, today was at home, with his Indian wife and

177

children, far up the Missouri. But in the handsome stone house on the hill the mayor of St. Louis made the Americans welcome.

There was a little ceremony in the public square. The French flag came down, the Stars and Stripes took its place. Captain Stoddard spoke to the people, assuring them that all their rights would be preserved. They could continue in their religion, their language, and their local government. Nothing would be changed, except that from this day on they would be American citizens. He hoped that they would be loyal and happy citizens of their new country.

Captain Stoddard sat down, and the crowd waited. Their mayor would speak for them.

He stood on the steps of his stone house, a dignified, handsome man past fifty. Gravely he thanked the American captain for his assurances. The people of St. Louis were satisfied that the promises would be kept. They knew that President Thomas Jefferson always kept his word.

As for themselves, the mayor went on, Captain Stoddard could say this to President

Jefferson. The people of St. Louis had always been loyal Frenchmen. Now, since the two governments had decided their future, they were content. The people of St. Louis, in every word and deed, would show themselves loyal Americans.

He spoke for all the people of St. Louis, and he had a right to do so. Mayor Auguste Chouteau had earned that right. From that first St. Valentine's Day, through all the years that had passed and for years to come, he never ceased to serve the city he loved. In the great modern city of today, no name is more tenderly remembered than that of Auguste Chouteau, Frenchman, American, first citizen of St. Louis.